The Magnificent Mind of

Ostaf

by

Jason T. Shapiro

Bob,
I Hope you're feeling good!
Enjoy this book. It's my
favorite one I've
written!
Best.
Jason

TREE
MOUTH
BOOKS

Published by **TREE MOUTH Books**, an imprint of:

Peter Weisz Publishing, LLC
7143 Winding Bay Lane
West Palm Beach, FL 33412 USA
www.peterweiszpublishing.com

Shapiro, Jason T., February, 2021
      The Magnificent Mind of Ostaf / Jason T. Shapiro
      Memoir — Biography — Nostalgia — Self-Help — Personal Improvement

ISBN: 9 781716 184833

Printed in the United States of America by Lulu.com.
1 2 3 4 5 6 7 8 9 10

Page design and cover design by Peter Weisz Publishing, LLC, West Palm Beach, FL
www.peterweiszpublishing.com

To Ryan and Alyssa:
Your creativity and disregard for failure
inspires me.
Never stop dreaming and believing.

Contents

Preface

I have always been fascinated with the dreamers—those who actually believe their imagination is the fuel to create positive change in the world. The ones who go against the grain, follow a different path, and never let the doubt of others impede their journey. These are the people who inspired me to write this story.

Reaching back into the memory box of my own life, I quickly realized I was subconsciously creating characters that a part of me already knew. I wrote this story based on relationships from my past that are worth sharing, with the intention of inspiring others.

There is a story behind the curtain of *every* person's life. My hope is that this book will prompt readers to be more conscious and consider that people's personalities are molded by their circumstances. The depth of one's turmoil often is not visible. When we can replace judgment with compassion, that is the true definition of kindness.

Regardless of political or religious views, we can all agree that there has never been a better time to see the good in humanity. It is there: we just need to look behind the curtain.

The Magnificent Mind of Ostaf

Chapter One

An Outcast Voyage

Our imagination is the gift used to create the vision of a dream, without any limitation of failure. The belief that something is possible before it has manifested into fruition, is the recipe to change the world.

• Harding, New Jersey – Saturday, June 26, 1993 •

Hey, Dad, what's going on?" Jacob smells food as he attempts to dart past his father. He's holding his black backpack. It's stuffed with cassette tapes, VHS movies, and random 1980s sports cards.

Howard spins around on his bar stool. He's wearing only underwear, and he's holding a deli bag full of corned beef. "Where are you going, Jakester? You know once you start college next month, you're not gonna be able to sleep until 12 o'clock every day. Ya got it?"

"I'm going to be 18 years old in a week. Stop already, big guy. Trust me, I know what I have to do." He pauses. "Dad, what's that over there?" Jacob prepares for the heist.

Howard glances at the random location across the room before realizing he's been set up. Jacob reaches inside the deli bag and snatches a handful of Howard's mouthwatering corned beef. Frustrated, Howard pokes Jacob in the stomach and shouts, "Keep your paws out of my food! Ya hear me?"

Jacob chuckles as he chomps on the prize. "You *always* fall for that one. That was delicious."

"Where are you heading off to? Please tell me you aren't going over to Ostaf's dump. He's nothing but trouble, Jake. I've told you that a *million* times…and you better not be giving him more of your things to sell. I'm serious about that." Howard clears his throat and turns his back.

Jacob jumps to Ostaf's defense. "Give him a break, Dad. He means well. You know he can't keep a job. I'm just trying to help him out."

"Jake-man, I admire the type of person you are, but remember this… sometimes people can't be helped, no matter how hard you try. You are wasting your time. I'm trying to help you here."

As Jacob hurries toward the front door he clenches his fists and snaps back, "I'll take my chances, Dad! I will call you later." Before leaving, he stands still and glares at his father. "You know, I'm getting *really* tired of you always ripping on him."

"Wise up, man!" Howard shouts, just as Jacob slams the front door closed.

My name is Jacob Roth. I'm the adult who was the 17-year-old boy you just met. When you see text inside a gray box like this, you will know it's me speaking to you in the current time. I'll pop in every so often and provide context and perspective on what you just read. Think of me as your tour guide as you embark on this journey with me. I am grateful you decided to read my story. Thank you, and welcome to "The Magnificent Mind of Ostaf."

Jacob opens the driver's-side door of his white, pristine 1984 Mercury Cougar. He gets in and starts the engine. He rolls down the windows and inserts a cassette labeled, "Old School Mix-Tape." Static blares through the speakers before his favorite song, "In Your Eyes" by Peter Gabriel, begins to play. Turning up the volume, Jacob backs out of the driveway. He sings along with it as the wind blows through his just-styled hair.

After cruising through town, Jacob reaches the on-ramp for the highway. He continues to belt out several more 1980s classic hits as if he were performing live on stage. After 30 minutes of therapeutic road time, Jacob exits off the highway. He passes miles of abandoned farmland before turning onto a dusty dirt road. Driving next on gravel and rocks, the popping sound from the car's rubber tires drowns out the music. Wobbling, the car continues down the uneven surface. Jacob grips the wheel with both hands. Beads of sweat drip down his temples. Captivating streams of water flow along both sides of the narrow lane. Jacob approaches the weathered and rotted remains of a wooden bridge. He pumps the brakes until he comes to a complete stop.

Jacob turns off the engine and steps out of the car. He hears the crunching gravel beneath his feet as he moseys along the trail. He gazes at the euphoric view of the forest surroundings. Several deer bustle through the leaf debris that blankets the ground. The chirping sound of blue jays and robins echoes through the clusters of enormous oak and pine trees. Jacob bends down, picks up a small rock and chucks it into the stream below the bridge as he crosses it. After a second of free fall, there's a splash.

Anytime I wanted to go to my Uncle O's house… and I use the term "house" very loosely, it was an adventure just to get there. No one else could locate him, even if they wanted to. I was one of the few people who knew where he lived. He had moved all over the country. Somehow, he ended up out in the boonies about 45 minutes away from my father, his older brother. You would have thought this was a wonderful thing, but unfortunately it wasn't.

Have you ever tried to push two large same-pole magnets together? It's impossible. You can't do it. There is something called *repulsion* that's an invisible force pushing the magnets away from each other. That's probably the best way to describe the toxic relationship between these two men.

My father was never happy to hear I was going to visit my uncle. Me, on the other hand? I looked forward to it. I enjoyed making the drive out west to the sticks. It gave me a chance to clear my head and reset. I know that probably sounds odd coming from someone who was only 17 at the time. I can vividly remember the feeling of calmness running through my body on the way to see him. I would play my favorite music, roll down the windows, and let the wind blow through my hair. Even though I risked my life crossing that bridge *(I'm laughing)* to see my uncle, it was worth it. I loved him…a lot.

Jacob's heartbeat races as he walks across the unstable structure. Each deep, gulping breath helps calm his nerves. With the same uncertainty as balancing on a tightrope, Jacob closes his eyes and whispers an impromptu prayer: "Almighty God, please don't let me fall through this piece of garbage bridge." Jacob is hopeful his prayer will help protect him from dropping through the rickety, decayed platform. Every soft, timid step inches him closer to victory. Finally, he crosses the finish line and completes what should have been a relaxing stroll across the 20-foot overpass. Jacob sighs and wipes the sweat from his forehead using the bottom of his T-shirt. He grins and shouts with tremendous relief, "Holy shit!" Shaking his head, he looks at his watch and starts the trek up the dirt road.

The squirrels shoot through the roughage as Jacob passes corroded household appliances that have been discarded and are littered along the sides of the path. In the distance he sees the run-down, mid-1920s house. The beams holding up the front porch overhang are slightly tilted. There is a large blue tarp draped across the roof, covered with pockets of water collected from the rainstorm the evening before. Several second-story windows are boarded up with decayed plywood. The asbestos shingle siding is coated with mold and clumps of green algae. The shrubs surrounding the perimeter of the home are overgrown, blocking sunlight from the windows. A 1975 AMC Gremlin is parked in front of the garage. Its yellow paint has faded and the body is riddled with severe rust holes. A trash bag is taped over the passenger's side window to prevent rain from entering.

The sun's intense summer rays pound down from the clear, majestic, blue sky. The humidity is thick and sticky. Jacob continues to wipe the extreme perspiration from his face onto the bottom of his damp T-shirt. He approaches the porch steps and stands on each one with caution. The creaking sound of the rotted wood makes Jacob uneasy. He attempts to avoid the rusty nails sticking out from the loose boards. He pulls open the rickety screen door and knocks on the door. He peeks around and notices a gray tabby cat curled up and snoozing on a rocking chair. Despite Jacob's knocking a few times, there is no answer.

Through the window's empty panes, Jacob shouts, "Are you home? It's me. Open up!" Losing his patience, he opens the front door. It's unlocked and Jacob wanders inside. The stench of rotten garbage and filth immediately fills his nostrils.

"Oh my God, it smells so bad," Jacob mumbles to himself. The house is dark and clutter is visible on every surface, in every direction. As Jacob maneuvers around piles of dirty clothing and sealed cardboard boxes, he shouts again, "Are you here?" Continuing through the room, he shuffles between collections of antique furniture pieces stacked one on top of another. Tools and appliance parts are scattered across the floor. The kitchen sink is overflowing with food-encrusted pots and pans. Jacob hears an AM news broadcast playing from a transistor radio. He follows the sound and creeps inside the cave-like bedroom.

An obese man with a scruffy, graying beard is lying on his back, wearing only boxer shorts. He's sleeping on a stained tweed couch, snoring while his glasses slide on and off his face. A lit cigarette is burning in the ceramic ash tray. Jacob glances over to the corner of the room where he sees a large crock pot with battery-operated fans glued onto the sides. It is sitting on top of a flimsy, foldable card table. Jacob lifts the top off of the pot. There are blue ice cartridges attached using Velcro tape on the inside.

"So, you found the invention that is going to revolutionize the ice cream industry?" the man blurts out, coughing.

Jacob is startled from the unexpected greeting. "Hey, I thought you were sleeping?"

The man responds, "I was, but you woke me up, asshole. I was up all night working on that masterpiece. It took me hours to design and build the prototype. Actually, I have to call the CEO of Carvel today and set up an appointment. I'm telling you…I am going to sell millions of those."

"What exactly does it do?" Jacob wonders as he inspects the world's next great invention.

Hacking and wheezing, the man answers, frustrated, "Are you kidding me? What does it do? Dude, that machine right there will keep your ice cream frozen for literally hours. Imagine you're having a summer barbecue and you want to bring ice cream. Leaving it in the carton, it will be soup within five minutes. If you have the *Cream Cooler*, just put the carton inside and you're set for the entire day! It only weighs 10 pounds."

"That sounds awesome. Hopefully you sell lots of them," Jacob encourages.

Insulted, the man answers while trying to catch his breath, "Hopefully? Are you kidding me? I *will* sell millions of them."

"That's great, Uncle O. Believe me, I hope you do. What ever happened with the vacuum that had the built-in drink holder and radio?" Jacob inquires.

"The *Utility Vac*? Yeah, that was a winner…if only the CEO of Hoover would have gotten back to me." He picks up the lit cigarette from the ashtray and takes a long drag on it. "So, what have you been up to, Dude?"

"Oh, not much. You know, this is the last summer I have before I start college in the fall. The cool thing is that my friend Mitch is going to the same school I'll be going to."

Ostaf's mouth falls open. "Holy shit! College? I remember watching you run around in your diaper." He chuckles. "You know your mom and dad would never let me take you anywhere by myself. Your dad would always have to tag along. They never thought I was *capable* of taking care of you. Screw them both."

Jacob takes a deep breath and runs his fingers through his hair. "Hey, I brought you some items to sell at the flea market this weekend. I think you might be able to get some decent money out of this stuff."

"Thanks, but I don't need your crap. I'm not the *loser* your father thinks I am. I've done fine for myself over the years," Ostaf proclaims.

Jacob glances at the trash-infested house and then stares at his uncle struggling to get up off the raunchy couch.

"You're a good kid, Jacob. I'm sorry, I don't mean to take my frustrations out on you. Let's go into the kitchen. I'll make us some breakfast. I think I have some eggs and cereal left."

Jacob is confused. *Breakfast? It's 2:30 in the afternoon.*

They both dart around the clutter and head into the kitchen. Sitting down in one of the chairs, Jacob is quick to catch his balance as it sways from side to side.

Ostaf chooses a pan from the collection in the sink. "Oh, be careful on that chair: one of the legs is loose. Listen, these eggs expired last week, but they should still be good. How many do you want?"

Jacob cringes. "Um, I'll have one. Thanks." He stares at the filthy countertops and appliances. "Hey Uncle O, would you ever want me to help you clean up your house? I mean, I have the next few weeks off. I'm happy to help. I could trim the bushes outside and fix the porch steps. We could get this place looking sweet. I can even ask Mitch to help us."

"Thanks, but I'm happy with the way it looks. I don't need help. Everything is just the way I want it. Do you want a beer with your eggs?" Uncle O asks while coughing. He twists the cap off and sets it down next to Jacob. "Hey, when we're done, let's go down into the basement. I'll show you some other cool stuff I'm working on. I have a new theory on time travel. I know you love the movie *Back to the Future*, so it may interest you. You've heard of Albert Einstein, right?" Jacob awaits the punch line. "Well, there was an important piece to Einstein's time travel theory that he was missing. I figured it out."

Jacob humors his uncle. "Wow, really? That's amazing. I have always been fascinated with time travel. It would be a trip to see my parents as teenagers. But yeah, I'd love to hear about that one some time, Doc Brown."

"Good one, Dude. By the way, your father was no angel in high school. Anyway, there's so much shit I have down in that basement. I have million-dollar ideas scattered all over the place. I just need someone who wants to buy them. Maybe you can ask your dad if he could invest in some of this stuff with me." The silence is uncomfortable. "He owes me, Jacob!" Ostaf slams his fist on the table.

Looking at the clock, Jacob stutters, "Uh, sure…yeah, I'll ask him and see what he says. Listen, I have to get going."

"What about your breakfast?" Ostaf takes a swig from the opened beer bottle and then clears the mucus from his throat.

Jacob can sense the tension escalating. "Can I take a rain check? I'll be back next week. I have more stuff in my closet for you."

Reaching into his backpack, Jacob pulls out a plastic bag and places it on the table. "Like I told you, there's some good stuff in here. Make sure you go this week and sell it. I even threw in some of my best baseball cards. You'll see there's a Ken Griffey Jr. rookie card I found. You can get at least $50 for it. Oh, and I'm giving you my autographed Lyle Alzado card. It's in the bag, too."

Ostaf takes off his glasses and picks the crust out of his eyes. "Dude, I'm not taking that. It's your favorite card." He peers into the bag. "Why the hell are you so good to me? You're really the *only* person in my life that gives a shit about how I'm doing."

"'Cause you're my uncle. That alone makes you cool," Jacob laughs as he zips up his backpack. "Listen, like I said, I will be by next week and we are going to do some summer cleaning. We're going to get this place looking good. Have an awesome week, OK? I love ya."

Coughing up phlegm, Ostaf spits onto his plate. "Love you, too, bud. Enjoy the rest of your day."

Although he is repulsed, Jacob looks at the mucus and notices small blood droplets within the saliva. He gets up, hugs his uncle, and starts walking toward the front door. Making his way past the obstacles of trash, Jacob finally exits the house and begins the voyage back to his car.

So that was my Uncle O. Let's just say there was always something "unique" about him. Even when I was a young child, I remember something wasn't quite right. He was different than everyone else in the family. Like a gigantic kid. He was always loving and kind to me, but "off." I guess most families have that one relative no one quite gets. The crazy thing is that for some reason, in the case of Uncle O, I did get him.

At that point, my uncle was only 44 years old—actually, the same age I am today. However, if I'm being honest, he looked 64. It was clear he wasn't aging well. I could tell his health was going to catch up to him if he didn't start taking care of himself. Even though he was relatively young, I still worried about him. I may have been the only one in the family who felt that way. My father had absolutely no patience for him…none. They were oil and water. My father always worked hard for everything he had and my uncle always felt that my dad *owed* him something. All my uncle ever wanted was for my father to be proud of him. It was a dysfunctional relationship and oftentimes I was caught right in the middle of it.

Chapter Two

Lovestruck

• The Next Day •

The roaring sound of a vacuum thuds against Jacob's bedroom door. His eyes flash wide open and he is awakened from a deep sleep. He looks at the digital clock that displays it is 7:30 a.m. Infuriated, he grits his teeth and then grumbles, "Jesus Christ. You gotta be kidding."

Pounding his fist on the mattress, Jacob gets dressed before stomping out of his room to confront the cleaning lady. He yanks the vacuum cord from the wall outlet. "Are you *really* serious right now? It's 7:30 in the morning. I'm exhausted." Jacob is losing his patience as he pleads his case.

The woman answers with a thick Polish accent, "I am sorry, honey, your mother told me to start the vacuuming first, before I do anything else."

Jacob groans as he marches into Linda's bedroom. "Are you kidding me, Mom? You basically told the cleaning lady to wake me up at 7:30 in the morning? I was up late last night."

"If you don't like it, you can move out at any time." Jacob bites his lip. "And why were you up so late, anyway? Please don't tell me you were rummaging through your closet again looking for things to give that moronic uncle of yours." Linda's posture stiffens as she turns away.

The tension escalates as Jacob snaps back, "What the hell did he ever do to you? I swear you just repeat *everything* Dad says. Uncle O has no one. You *all* should be ashamed of how nasty you are to him."

Howard overhears the argument brewing as he re-enters the house after getting the Sunday paper. "What's going on? I could hear your screeching voice from outside, Jake."

"I'm getting really tired of everyone giving me crap because I actually care about Uncle O. The guy is in rough shape, but of course no one gives a shit. The worst part, Dad...you're his freakin' older brother!" Jacob loses control of his emotions and scolds his father.

Howard chucks the newspaper against the wall and fires back. "You don't know anything about the situation, Jacob! That guy is nothing but trouble. He will ruin your life, just like he's ruined everyone else's. Wise up and listen to me. I've told you a *million* times...you-are-wasting-your-time!"

"I'm not listening to this, Dad. I'm leaving. I'll see you guys later!" Jacob shouts as he speed walks to the kitchen counter. He grabs his car keys and slides on his sneakers.

Howard asks, "Where are you going? You didn't even eat breakfast."

"I'm going to Mitch's. I'll eat at his house. I need to get out of here," Jacob shouts as he opens the front door, flings it closed, and charges outside. He hurries down the driveway. Howard's newly polished, silver Jaguar Vanden Plas is blocking Jacob's car. Irritated, Jacob gets into his Cougar and tears into the middle of the front yard. As he reverses, sunken tire tracks are left in the grass. Jacob's car drops off the curb and then speeds away. The smell of burnt rubber fills the air.

After a short trip down the street, Jacob pulls into an open, gated driveway. He slams the car into park, gets out, walks toward the front door and rings the doorbell. Jacob taps his foot as he waits for someone to answer. The door cracks open and an attractive woman in her mid-40s sashays outside. She leans in. "Hi honey, how are you? You look *so much older* every time I see you. What's the matter? You seem upset. Are you OK?"

"Hi, Ms. Glantz. I'm fine. My parents are just giving me a hard time, that's all." He swallows and fiddles with his car keys.

She rubs Jacob's shoulder. "Oh, I'm sorry, sweetie. I'm sure your mom and dad are just looking out for you.... Oh, and *how many times* have I told you to call me Julie?"

"Um, thanks...Julie. I appreciate the concern. I'm just going to go find Mitch, if that's OK," Jacob mutters as his voice cracks. The interaction becomes awkward and a perspiration mustache begins to form on his upper lip. Jacob wipes away the sweat and rushes inside the house. Ms. Glantz grins from behind.

After walking through the kitchen, Jacob sees a foldable, wooden ladder hanging down from the ceiling inside the hallway. He climbs the steps to the top and enters the loft. The decor consists almost exclusively of New Jersey Nets memorabilia. Custom-framed jerseys and photographs fill the walls. Lucite cases containing autographed basketballs are displayed on wooden pedestals. They are placed in each corner of the recreation room. Jacob walks past the pool table toward the enormous 65-inch television. There is a red-haired teenager lounging on a beanbag wearing head-phones as he plays a video game. The graphics on the television screen are like nothing Jacob has ever seen.

"Hey!" Jacob shouts as he grabs the boy's shoulders from behind.

The boy shrieks, "What the hell, dick!" as he pushes Jacob.

"Dude, are you fuckin' kidding me? Is that the PlayStation? It's not supposed to come out until next December...in Japan!" Jacob steps closer and squints. "Wait a minute...please don't tell me you're actually playing Final Fantasy VI." Jacob tries to contain his excitement.

"Yeah, it is. My dad knows the vice president of retail sales for Sony. They sponsored the slam dunk contest when it was here in Jersey. I think it was back in the early 80s. They sat next to each other that weekend. My dad gets him great deals on cars, so he gives my dad shit before it even hits the retail market. That reminds me, are you going with me to the Nets' team dinner next week? It's going to be awesome. Kenny and Derrick will be there, I found out."

"Sure, I'll go. That sounds fun. And, by the way...I wouldn't tell *anyone* you have that PlayStation. It's like having a million dollars cash inside your house," Jacob advises as he admires the gaming system.

That's my boy Mitch. We were best friends since preschool and were practically like brothers. Our birthdays were only a few weeks apart. We also happened to live in the same neighborhood in Harding. Here's the deal: this kid was an absolute genius. He memorized every single volume of the *Encyclopedia Britannica.* I remember when we were in sixth grade, he built a freakin' *working* computer out of parts we found at my dad's office and one trip to Radio Shack. Not only could he build computers, but he could also program them. His parents wanted him to be an engineer, but Mitch's dream was to be a doctor one day.

Our families became good friends over the years. We would go on cruises and vacations together. It was like having a second family. It was great while it lasted. Unfortunately, back in 1988, Mitch's older brother, Jeff, passed away from a drug overdose. He was only 17 when he died. His parents' relationship was already on rocky ground prior to that horrific incident, and after a while, the agony of losing Jeff pushed them to divorce. The only good thing for Mitch and his mother was that his dad was rich. He owned over 30 incredibly successful car dealerships in the tristate area. Mitch had everything he wanted, including courtside seats for every single New Jersey Nets home game. His father sold the owner of the team his cars and they became good friends. Mitch didn't really care about money; in fact, he hated driving around in his brand-new black convertible Lexus. He would always say, "A dream is worth a million dollars and believing you can actually achieve it is like winning the lottery." His intellect was way beyond his years. We knew each other better than our own parents knew us. He was the brother I never had and I was a substitute for the one he wished was still alive.

"So, what the hell is going on, Jake? You look pissed off." Mitch can sense that something happened. He turns off his gaming system and television with the remote control.

Jacob's overcome with emotion. "I saw my Uncle O yesterday. He's a mess, man."

"What do you mean? I thought you said last time you went there he was doing better. Wasn't he selling stuff at that flea market in town and starting to make some money?" Mitch puts on his sneakers.

Taking a deep breath, Jacob explains, "It's not even about the money. He would never tell me, but I know my grandmother gives him just enough to pay his bills. Although, who knows what he does with it. Anyway, it wouldn't matter if he was a millionaire. He just doesn't know how to do basic life tasks. It's like it doesn't register. His house…it looks like an episode from the television show *Sanford and Son*. There is shit *everywhere*. I could barely walk through each room. God only knows what his basement looks like. It's his 'laboratory' where he builds his inventions and keeps all his 'million dollar' theories and hypotheses." Jacob chuckles.

"Don't they say that there is a fine line between being insane and being a genius?" The boys laugh in unison. "Last time we saw your uncle I remember him telling us about the 'Super Straw' where you could drink your soda from another room," Mitch reminisces as he grabs a cue stick. He mocks the wacky invention by pretending it's a straw.

Jacob flops onto the futon. "Yeah, I know. He comes up with some stupid shit. I try to be supportive each time he tells me about his newest contraption, but it's not easy. When I saw him yesterday, he showed me a portable ice cream cooler built out of a fuckin' crock pot." Jacob puts his hands behind his head and stares at the ceiling. "You know, a part of me wonders if he actually had the hustle and work ethic, could he sell one of his prototypes? There's investors out there looking to make a quick buck." Jacob stands up and starts to pace. "I mean, what if…? What if something down in that basement actually could be something?"

Mitch shrugs. "Anything is possible, I guess. You never know, but it sounds like he needs to get his life straightened out first and foremost. I mean, he's still young. There's time."

"I guess. It's so weird. I still can't figure out exactly why my dad and uncle can't stand each other. All my dad ever says is to stay away from him. He is going to ruin my life like he did to everyone else. Something is missing there. It just doesn't make sense." Jacob ponders as he rolls the 8 ball across the pool table. It drops into the corner pocket.

Mitch cracks his knuckles and looks at the clock. "I don't know, man…but what I do know is that I am starving. You want to hit up Bagel Land?"

"Dude, you don't have to ask me twice. Aren't the free mini muffins the best? I could eat them all day. Hopefully we can sneak out before your mom sees me." Jacob smiles as he playfully pokes the side of Mitch's belly.

Mitch doesn't appreciate the humor. "Don't be an ass." He puts Jacob in a head lock and gives him a nuggie.

The boys scamper out of the house and get into Mitch's car. The song "Give It Away" by the Red Hot Chili Peppers is on the radio. Jacob turns up the volume and begins to sing the song as if he were auditioning for the band. Moments later, the car pulls into a parking spot in front of Bagel Land.

Mitch gasps. "Oh, shit! Look whose car that is! She's here! I can't believe it. You better not be a pussy, and go and talk to her."

Jacob glances over in anticipation. He sees a polished, apple-red convertible BMW with the top down. "I'll see, man. That may not even be her car. It's not like there aren't a hundred red convertible BMWs in this town." Jacob rubs the back of his neck and then begins to bite his fingernails.

Mitch jokes, "And they all have our high school mascot painted on the window with the class of '93?" He tugs Jacob's shirt to get his attention. "Christine is here, Dude. She likes you. Stop being so damn shy."

Jacob clears his throat and tries to gather his composure. "Let's just go eat. If I see her, I'll say hi. You better not embarrass me. I'm serious. I have a reputation to uphold."

"A reputation? Don't you have to date girls to have a reputation? Please stop, you're making me cry, I am laughing so hard." Mitch slaps his knee.

Annoyed, Jacob begins to lose his patience. "Let's go in and eat already. I gotta get going soon. Remember, if we see Christine, keep it cool."

The boys stroll into Bagel Land and sit down at the table. They start to devour the basket of assorted mini muffins. "Where do you have to go today? It's Sunday morning. Be thankful we stopped going to Hebrew school years ago," Mitch reminds Jacob, chuckling.

I'm thinking about driving out to see my Uncle O again. I haven't been in his basement in a long time. Believe it or not, there is some cool shit to look at down there. Once school starts, I won't be seeing him often. I need to try and spend as much time as possible with him now." Jacob scoops out the crumbs from the basket.

With a warm, welcoming smile, the waitress swoops over and greets the boys with a distinct South Jersey accent: "Good mornin'. Do ya know what you want, or should I bring ya a menu?"

Out of nowhere, Jacob, pops off of his chair and slams his hands onto the table. "I'll get whatever he's having!" In a frenzy, he dashes in the direction of the bathroom.

Confused but starving, Mitch requests, "We will take two orders of the Sunday Special, please. Oh, and can we get a refill on the mini muffins?"

Without warning, a teenage girl wearing rolled-up denim shorts and an oversized gray sweatshirt sits down in Jacob's chair. As she smiles, kindness radiates across the table. Her crystal-blue eyes sparkle, hypnotizing Mitch as he gazes at her. The blonde highlights in her long, wavy brown hair shine bright like her captivating spirit. Gentleness and compassion flow from each word she speaks.

Mitch stutters as he welcomes the girl. "Hey, how are you? When did you get here? I had no idea you liked this place." Beads of sweat begin to percolate on his forehead.

In a sweet tone, the girl begins, "Things are good. I'm here with Lisa. We're just getting ready to leave." She looks around. "Where did Jacob go? I saw him make a beeline toward the bathroom."

"Oh, yeah…that," Mitch attempts a response.

The girl questions, "Is he OK?"

"I think so. Listen, please don't say anything. The eggs didn't agree with him, but you didn't hear that from me," Mitch mischievously whispers to the girl. She covers her mouth and mumbles, "Oh my goodness."

From behind Mitch, Jacob approaches the table. "Oh…hey, Christine. How are you doing? I had no idea you were here," Jacob babbles as he uses a damp paper towel to wipe the sweat from his rose-colored face.

"I'm great. Sorry, I hope I'm not bothering you guys. I just wanted to stop by and say hi." Christine smiles as the waitress places the boys' food onto the table.

Jacob offers a swift assurance: "Oh, you're not bothering us. Trust me."

"Wow…a second side of eggs? You must be really hungry. Well…I gotta go," Christine informs. "We're heading down the shore today. It was good seeing you both. I hope you feel better, Jacob. Bye."

Perplexed, Jacob waves and replies, "Thanks," and then looks over at Mitch mouthing the words, "What-is-she-talking-about?" Christine frolics away and Jacob glares from across the table. "What the hell did you tell her, Mitch?"

"Um, nothing." He folds his hands and whistles. "Fine, maybe I told her the eggs didn't exactly agree with you. Sorry, I couldn't help myself," Mitch confesses through snide chuckles.

Jacob clenches his teeth. "You mean the eggs I never ate, asshole? You totally embarrassed me. What did I tell you right before we walked inside?"

Without warning, Christine returns. "You may need these. I could see you're sweating." She hands Jacob a stack of napkins and then dashes away.

"Oh, thanks!" Jacob shouts across the crowded restaurant. Everyone stares at him. Looking down, he sees a message written on the top napkin. It says, "call me sometime" with Christine's phone number and a smiley face.

Mitch's eyes widen as he presses his palms against his cheeks. "Holy shit!" He stares at the message. Everyone in the restaurant looks over again. "Jake, do you know what this means?"

"She needs a study partner?" Jacob's naive response is comical.

Mitch leans in. "She wants to study alright, and it has nothing to do with school." He pretends to faint. "Christine Dupree just gave you her telephone number and told you to call her. It doesn't get clearer than that."

"I don't know. I'll have to see." Jacob's nerves get the best of him and he knocks the stack of napkins onto the ground.

Mitch is stunned when he notices Jacob's empty plate. "You're already done eating? Did you inhale your eggs? I haven't even taken a bite of mine yet."

"Well, you eat like a snail, bro. Hurry up. I want to get over to my uncle's before it gets too late." Jacob reaches down and grabs the sacred napkin from the floor. He folds it up and places it onto the table.

Shoveling his food into his mouth, Mitch mumbles, "Do you want me to go with you? I haven't seen the big guy in a while. I could use a laugh."

"Sure, if you're up to it. Just don't get upset when he calls you Red Head Fred." The boys both laugh. "He's always liked you, Dude. Hey, remember the time at my Bar Mitzvah when he got drunk and tried to convince your mom that Steven Spielberg offered him a multi-script deal to write his next two movies...and the best part was that he would co-direct them?" Jacob reminisces.

Flagging down the waitress for the check, Mitch laughs. "Yeah, I remember that. I also remember him and your dad getting into a tussle during the horah. Everyone was dancing and singing, and they were in the middle of the circle arguing. Man, it got heated for sure. The crazy thing is that no one would even know they were brothers, other than their appetites, of course."

"That horah argument is on video. My mom was so embarrassed. I remember my dad's other brother, Dan, and my freakin' grandma had to break it up. Jesus, Dude. My family is so fuckin' dysfunctional. Sometimes I wonder if I was adopted." Jacob shakes his head and sighs.

Mitch reaches over and pats Jacob's back. "Well, don't get down in the dumps, bro. Everyone's family has their own issues. Hell, I know mine does. My mom can barely get through a day without crying. Here take this," he reminds Jacob, tossing him the holy napkin with Christine's phone number on it.

Gasping, Jacob realizes he almost forgot it. "Jeez, thanks. I would have left it here. I'm a total mess, man. My heart rate still hasn't gone back down. Hey, be honest: do you think she really likes me?"

"Shut up. I'm not playing this game anymore," Mitch tosses a hand full of sugar packets at Jacob. "Let's get going to your uncle's. I remember it takes forever to get there." The boys pay their tab at the register and leave. After getting into Mitch's car, they roll the windows down, turn up the radio, and head out on the quest to Ostaf's house.

Chapter Three

The Bridge to Kindness

After 30 minutes of driving, they veer onto the dirt road. The tires crunch the gravel and pebbles before they park and exit the car.

"Shit, I totally forgot about that rickety, decaying bridge. It's like walking across a platform of Popsicle sticks. It even looks more run-down since the last time I was here. How does your uncle ever leave this place? He'd fall right through it," Mitch sneers.

Jacob lowers his shoulders in a show of sadness. "He never leaves." Both boys are silent. They stare at the bridge as they exit the car.

"Ok, I'm just gonna run across it as fast as I can with my eyes closed." Mitch bends down to tie his sneakers and then stretches his hamstrings. Suddenly, he takes off like a cheetah. He blasts across the unstable, decimated structure. Jacob yells, "Dude, my grandma runs faster than you!"

Just as Mitch approaches the last few feet of the bridge, his back foot penetrates the decaying plywood. He falls to the ground as blood starts to seep from the scrapes on his ankle and calf. Mitch shrieks for help as he attempts to push himself up.

Jacob's body tremors. "I'm coming—hang on! Try not to move." He races toward his best friend. As Jacob approaches, the pressure of Mitch using his other leg to push himself up causes the platform to lift up off the nails.

"I can't get any closer! My weight is gonna cause the entire support to flip up!" Jacob cautions.

With anxiety evident on his face, Mitch begs for help as he's frozen with fear. "FUCKIN' HELP ME, DUDE!"

"I can't go any further. Hang on, man!" Jacob squeezes his eyes closed as he inches toward Mitch. His breathing becomes shallow and his hands shake.

Just as the platform begins to rise higher into the air, a massive hand reaches down from the sky and snatches Mitch by the back of the collar of his shirt. The unknown hand hoists Mitch high into the air, like a rag doll, and then whips him off the bridge. His bloodied leg is free and the platform crashes into the ravine below.

Tears blurring his vision, Mitch stares up into a scruffy, graying beard. As he pushes a massive cluster of hair to the side, Mitch looks through the man's thick glasses and can see the eyes of kindness. "Uncle O?" Mitch asks as he smiles with relief.

Setting Mitch down, Ostaf scolds the boys. "What the hell are you idiots doing crossing this bridge? Did you not notice this thing was ready to come crashing down any day now? Morons, I tell you. It's like you two share one brain." He throws his hands in the air.

"How am I going to get across?" Jacob screams as he begins to edge backward toward the car.

Ostaf is irate and reprimands his nephew: "Jesus Christ, Jacob! All you had to do was ask me." He scratches his nostril with his finger. "Just walk into the woods over there. Do you see that *other* bridge over by that log cabin?" Ostaf points. "Well, that's the one you need to use when you come to see me. Not this piece of shit that was built a hundred years ago!"

"Holy fuck! You saved my life. I was minutes away from being fish bait," Mitch screeches as he wraps his arms around Ostaf's leg. He winces at Ostaf's decaying toenails.

Jacob scratches his head. "How did you know we were here?"

"Well, you sounded like two school girls crying for your mother on the first day of kindergarten. Butch up, guys." Ostaf lets out a belly laugh so intense that the squirrels nearby scamper away.

"Jesus, Uncle O, was that a laugh or thunder? I'll meet you guys at the house! I'm gonna go use the other bridge." Jacob exhales and checks his pulse.

"Don't get lost," Ostaf jokes as he scoops up Mitch like a bear cub and carries him away.

After a tranquil stroll through the woods and a successful walk across the *other* bridge, Jacob makes his way to his uncle's house. Walking up the dirt and gravel driveway, he sees Mitch sitting on a lawn chair. He is reclined, with a beer in the drink holder. His wounded leg is extended and propped up onto an eroded aluminum cooler. His injury has been treated with peroxide and is neatly wrapped in gauze. Mitch is holding an ice pack on his thigh.

Jacob walks up the porch steps. He does a double take and shuffles backwards. "Who cleaned you up like this?"

Mitch pretends to make a toast and then sips his beer. "Not only did your uncle save my life, but he took care of me like he was a freakin' medic. He doused my leg in more magic potions than a scientist. I feel great."

"Wow. That was really nice of him. See? My dad would never care if I told him a story like that. He would try and find all the negatives. Like, the fact you have a brewski sitting in the cupholder." Both boys laugh. "Listen, my uncle may be a *little* rough around the edges, but he has a good heart." Jacob's face lights up.

Mitch asks, "A *little* rough around the edges? Bro, his breath and beard smelled like rotten ass with beer mixed into it. Wait, that can be his next invention. A line of scented room sprays and candles that smell like piss."

"Hey! I heard that, punk! You're lucky I didn't leave your ass sitting on the bridge, Red Head Fred!" Uncle O shouts as he stumbles outside barefoot, smoking a cigarette. The smell of burning tobacco fills the air.

Mitch takes a swig of his beer. "I'm just messing with you, Big O. Have you heard of karma? Ya know…*what goes around comes around.* Something good will happen to you. I believe that."

"Nothing good ever happens to me. I can't catch a fuckin' break. You know how many of my inventions should be in people's houses… making me millions? Changing the world!" Ostaf takes a drag on his cigarette. He blows the smoke high into the air. "Did I ever tell you about the Fence Fitter? See that rusted chain-link fence over there?" Uncle O points. "Well, I made a gorgeous, beige vinyl covering that goes right over the top of it. Like a sandwich box. Then there are clasps that strap around the metal posts that are already cemented into the ground. A tornado couldn't budge it. Within a few hours of installation, it looks like a new fence, for half the price." Ostaf snaps his fingers like The Fonz. He sets his cigarette in the ashtray and hacks up a mouthful of mucus. The boys flinch as he spits over the railing. "Damn, look how far that went. Back in high school we would have a contest to see who could spit the furthest. Guess who won?" Ostaf sticks both thumbs up and points to himself. "Yours truly."

Jacob lowers his head. "Sorry I didn't bring you anything today, Uncle O. We were eating breakfast and decided to drive over here right from the bagel place."

"I don't need your shit, Dude. I make my own money. I'm not a child." Reaching over, he tries to give Jacob a wet willy. "So, did you buy me any bagels?" Ostaf's stomach growls.

Jacob shakes his head but offers to do a mitzvah. "Sorry, no bagels, but we can help you clean your house today."

Caught off guard, Mitch mumbles, "Clean his house? What the hell?" Then he changes the subject: "Hey, Uncle O…we ran into Christine at the bagel place!"

Ostaf simmers with curiosity. He sits down, inches the chair forward, and whispers…. "*The* Christine?"

"It was no big deal. We just bumped into each other." Jacob rocks in place with his hands inside his pockets.

Mitch begins to clap. "Oh…it was a big deal. Trust me. Tell your uncle what she gave you." He smiles from ear to ear. "Actually, why don't you just show him what she gave you."

Jacob struggles to contain his excitement. He reaches into his back pocket and pulls out the treasured script. He struts over to his uncle and hands him the napkin. Jacob sits down and puffs out his chest.

"She gave you a paper napkin? Congrats!" Ostaf uses it to wipe his runny nose.

As his face reddens, Jacob throws up his arms. "Whoa! What the hell are you doing? There's important information written on that, you idiot."

Puzzled, Ostaf unfolds the napkin. "What are you talking about? There's nothing on it except my snot."

Jacob snatches the napkin from his uncle's hand. Disgusted, he examines both sides. Panicking, Jacob yells out, "Fuck! He's right. There's nothing written down. I can't believe it."

"What are you talking about, Dude? She wrote down her number. It was on there. I saw it." Mitch confirms.

Jacob leans forward and covers his face with both hands. "When I accidentally knocked over the stack of napkins, I must have picked up the wrong one. I can't believe this, guys. After four years of waiting, she *finally* gave me her number, and I lost it. I could literally cry."

Suddenly, Jacob feels two massive hands grasp his shoulders. Ostaf tries to console his emotional nephew. "Sorry, Dude. That sucks…but if she gave you her digits, she likes you. It's simple: just tell her you lost her number and you need it again. Don't stress yourself out."

"You obviously don't know me. I am *totally* intimidated by her. Just the thought of walking up to Christine and telling her I lost her number gives me anxiety." Jacob takes a deep breath and massages his own temples.

Excited, Mitch hatches out a plan. "I got it! Here's what we do. We know she goes to that bagel joint. Next time we go, we bring your uncle and he walks over and gets her number for you."

"Jesus. You think I want to scare the shit out of her by sending over an old guy who looks like a bearded bounty hunter?" Jacob rolls his eyes and sighs. Without warning, Jacob is catapulted into the air while still seated on the chair. Adrenaline rushes through his body. "Holy shit! Put me down!" Jacob clenches the arm rests with all his might. "I'm sorry. Ok, fine, you don't look like a bearded bounty hunter. You look like a Viking." Uncle O begins to spin around as he hoists Jacob even higher.

After several minutes of the carnival ride, Ostaf lowers Jacob to the ground like the ending of an intense dance.

"Dude, watch it, or next time the chair goes flying…with you in it. Understand?" Ostaf makes his point as he attempts to put his sweaty, hairy underarm on Jacob's face.

Gagging, Jacob looks Ostaf in the eye and says: "Now I know the perfect gift to get you for your birthday."

"What's that? Your dad apologizing to me for being a dick-head?" Ostaf doesn't miss a beat. He picks up his cigarette from the ashtray and takes a deep puff.

Reaching around, Jacob pokes his uncle's obese belly and teases, "Um, no…a can of deodorant." The two younger men thought that was funny. "Let's go inside. I'm sweating my ass off out here," Jacob wailed.

Regardless of the topic of conversation, my uncle would always weave in the idea that my father should apologize to him. I never wanted to get involved, but I have to admit I was curious as to what he was talking about. Apologize for what? They had a deep-rooted dislike for each other as far back as I could remember. I tried asking my dad what caused the rift between them, but he never would give me an honest answer. His response was always about the traumatic stress my uncle, while growing up, inflicted on my grandparents. The whole thing never made sense. Especially because I knew my dad wasn't exactly the "golden child" himself. I heard plenty of *those* stories over the years from my grandmother. Either way, I continued to be in the middle of the feud and I was getting tired of it.

Everyone walks inside the dreary house. Upon entering, the stifling heat and humidity halts Mitch and Jacob in their tracks.

"It feels like a sauna in here!" Mitch can smell the mold permeating from the walls.

Ostaf apologizes and makes excuses for the situation. "Sorry. My air conditioning unit broke last night. I'll put a few fans on and open the windows. That should cool it off.

Mitch whispers to Jacob, "If we don't make it out of here alive, you were always my best friend. Oh, and I had a crush on Christine two years ago."

"Thanks for being honest, bro. That means a lot to me. I actually had a crush on your mom last year. It's important you know that before we perish from heat stroke," Jacob snaps back.

The boys navigate around the obstacle course of trash, clusters of furniture in various states of disrepair, and random mechanical parts. They make their way to the kitchen table as the sweat continues to simmer on their faces.

"So, what have you been working on, Big O?" Mitch asks as he uses his own T-shirt to wipe the perspiration off his face. There's no response. Jacob's uncle walks to the kitchen table and sits down. He coughs as he motions to the other chairs. "Take a seat, fellows." Ostaf's foul body odor fills the room.

Holding his breath, Mitch hustles to slide open the kitchen window. He can feel the sweat seeping through his shirt. Jacob darts over and turns on the battery-operated fan as the boys desperately attempt to increase the ventilation. They each sit down on the wobbly kitchen chairs.

Ostaf leans in. "Listen, guys, I'm not the *loser* everyone thinks I am. I have just had a lot of bad luck in my life. As the saying goes, "the chips never fell in my court." He scoops out the change in the ashtray and places it into his pocket. "Jacob, I was going to tell you this next time I saw you, but I know Mitch is like a member of the family." The boys scoot their chairs forward and their posture stiffens. A mild breeze flows through the house.

Tapping his fingers on the table, Ostaf begins to vent. "This shit has been bothering me for years. I have to get it off of my chest. It's important that you know, Jake. Please don't discuss this with your father. I don't need that asshole calling me up and yelling at me." He looks at his stack of unpaid bills. "Oh, wait, actually, he can't call me, my phone was disconnected."

From his timid tone, it is clear Jacob is caught off guard. "Yeah, I won't say anything. I promise. You know that anything we discuss doesn't leave this house."

Uncle O coughs and spills the beans. "I trust you, bud. I'm just going to say it. Your dad stole one of my ideas."

"Huh? What are you talking about? Which one? How do I not know this?" Jacob fires off a barrage of questions. Confused, he pulls his chair closer to his uncle.

Ostaf is harboring years of pent-up hostility. "Of course you don't know about this! Your father doesn't want anyone to have this information. Especially his own kid."

"So, what was it? How did it happen?" Jacob bites his nails.

Ostaf gets up and wanders over to the refrigerator. He grabs a beer and then sparks up another cigarette as soon as he sits back down. "It was October 27, 1987. It was spectacular outside. You know, the type of day where the brisk morning breeze shoots through the air and the red and gold leaves float down from the sky. The trees were bursting with every warm color on the palette. It looked like a Bob Ross painting. Anyhow, I was out on a stroll with a lovely gal I was dating. By the way, she was fuckin' gorgeous, guys. She was a well-known actress. That's another thing your dad was jealous of. I got all the chicks growing up and he would steal my sloppy seconds…but that's a story for another day."

Ostaf pretends to slap himself in the face. "Let me get back to the point here. So, I was trying to think of a way to eliminate the need for ice cubes in a plastic water bottle when out of nowhere, the idea pops into my dome. Actually, before I keep going, I have a question. What would happen if you poured a Coke into a water bottle filled with ice cubes?" Uncle O makes direct eye contact with both boys.

Mitch gives the logical answer. "You would have a water bottle filled with cold Coke?"

Ostaf responds, "Yes…and…what else?"

Jacob and Mitch rub their chins as they try to solve the sports drink bottle riddle.

"Dudes…come on! I thought you were going to be these smart college guys in the fall. Use your brains. You're going to have a plastic bottle filled with watered-down Coke from the ice melting."

Mitch makes it clear he is losing his patience. "Ok, so what was your invention? You're killing me, Smalls. I'll have graduated by the time you tell us."

"I'm getting to that. Chill out, my man. So, I rush to call my brother, Howard, and tell him I have this brilliant idea. Now, remember this is over six years ago, so we were on *slightly* better speaking terms. I explain that I had something I wanted to show him. Something that was "top secret," so I didn't want to discuss it on the phone. We met at his favorite deli in Livingston. Do you know that your father is *obsessed*

33

with good corned beef?" Ostaf can't help weaving the topic of food into his story.

Jacob nods and confirms, "Oh, yeah, I know. He eats it by the pound."

"Anyway, I pull out a drawing I had sketched in my basement." In mid-discussion, Ostaf gets up and moseys over to the bathroom. There is no sound of the door closing behind him.

Mitch is perplexed. "What the hell is he doing?"

"He's in his own world, bro. I guess he had to go to the bathroom," Jacob shrugs. "Oh, and *do not* touch his hands: he *never* washes them."

Mitch leans in and whispers, "Do you believe any of this stuff he tells you? He dated an actress? Your dad stole his idea?"

Jacob keeps his voice low. "Here's the deal. My uncle is one of those people who always exaggerates what really happened. Even I know that. But…buried in all of his stories there is a small amount of the truth. The part no one has patience for is trying to decipher what is fact or fiction."

The toilet flushes and Ostaf walks back and sits down at the table. "Sorry, fellas, I had to drop a deuce. I had a feeling that milk I drank earlier was sour. Anyway, where was I?"

Jacob, hiding his repulsion at those comments, reminds Ostaf, "Um, you pulled out a drawing that you sketched in your basement?"

"Oh, that's right. So, I had brought one of them architect tubes with me. Inside was the drawing. I unroll this big sheet of paper onto the table and I start to explain to your father what it was. As I mentioned before, I was trying to think of a way I could keep a drink cold without ice. Sounds impossible, right? Well…it's not. Now, one thing I *will* say is that your father has a great business mind. He is able to take an idea and bring it to life. From start to finish." Ostaf places a cigarette behind his ear. "Ok, other than ice cubes, what else would keep liquids cold?"

Mitch raises his hand and waves it in the air. "Dude, you're not in elementary school. You don't have to raise your hand. Jacob, where did you find this guy?" Ostaf's deafening laugh echoes through the house.

Mitch shouts the answer: "Blue ice packs! We put a few inside our cooler to keep our food cold when we go down the shore."

"Ah, why yes. You are correct, young Skywalker." Ostaf attempts to high-five Mitch without success. "You may be asking…well…how would one get a square-shaped blue ice pack inside a narrow sports drink bottle?" There is silence. "Ok, I will tell you: you can't. Here's the part that will blow your fuckin' mind." The boys stare at Ostaf as if he is revealing top secret government information. "On that sheet of paper I laid out on the table was the drawing that would change my life…or so I thought. I sketched out a narrow cylindrical cartridge filled with blue ice. It hung down from the top of the drinking bottle. In the cap, there was one hole for the straw and then a larger, threaded hole that the cartridge dropped into. It screwed perfectly into place." The boys look like they were just shown authentic photos of Bigfoot. "So, this unique-shaped blue ice cartridge was removable and could be placed inside the freezer when needed."

Jacob nods at his uncle with a slight grin. He mumbles in awe, "That's absolutely genius."

Mitch agrees. "The pure simplicity of it is what makes it so magnificent."

"So, how did my dad steal your idea?" Jacob stares into Ostaf's dejected eyes.

Ostaf struggles to harness his emotions. "Your father totally loved the idea. He thought it was a product we could quickly get patented and into production. You know Howard. Within the first five minutes, he was bursting with ideas. He was talking about all the different professional sports team logos we could license and slap on the bottle. I told him he could have the idea as long as he gave me 25 cents for every unit he sold."

"So, now you're a millionaire?" Mitch jokes and both boys look around the room.

Ostaf's eyes begin to bulge and his nostrils flare. Like an unexpected bolt of lightning, he strikes his fist on the table. "I haven't seen a fuckin' penny! I know he ended up getting them manufactured and is selling thousands in retail stores."

Mitch directs the question to Jacob. "Did you know about this? I gotta hear more of this story. This sounds interesting."

Jacob kicks Mitch's leg underneath the table. "Nope, I had no idea, but that is a crazy story." He checks his watch. "You know, Uncle O, I completely forgot. I told my dad I would meet him for lunch today. I really need to get going."

"Meet your dad for lunch?" Mitch is confused by the impromptu change of plans.

Jacob grits his teeth and reiterates, "Yes, Mitch, lunch with my dad. We try and do that every other Sunday. We enjoy spending time together." Kicking Mitch even harder, Jacob mouths the words, "Shut up."

"Come on, don't leave. I want to finish telling you the rest of the story. What the hell? It's important you know this." Ostaf gets up, walks over to the refrigerator and grabs another beer.

Jacob can sense the drama building. "Listen, I'll be back next week and you can finish telling me everything then. I promise. I also want to walk through the basement and see what's new down there."

Ostaf nods. "Ok. Sounds good, pal. Wait until I show you the *Sheet Sealer*. Hey, I got a question for you before you leave. How many times have you washed your clothing with your bed sheets? Then when you take the bed sheets out of the dryer, they are completely twisted with your shirts, pants, socks, all nestled in the elastic part? Like a giant ball and chain, that you have to untwist?"

"Um, I don't know. Mom won't let me do my own laundry. She says I'll break the machines." The blank expression on Jacob's face conceals his embarrassment.

Ostaf is shocked by the confession. "Bro, it's time to put on your big-boy pants already and do your own laundry. Does mommy still wipe your tuchus?" Everyone chuckles in unison. "Anyway, I came up with a washable netted bag that your sheets go into. Your clothes stay separated from your sheets and life is good."

"That's actually a great idea, Uncle O." Jacob gives a thumbs up and attempts to shuffle toward the door.

Ostaf proclaims his brilliance. "I'm an idea machine! I'll tell you more next time I see you." He raises his leg, passes gas, and smirks.

"Bye, Uncle O!" both boys shout as they hurry out of the house, holding their breath.

Mitch follows Jacob as they hike along the path and alternate bridge that leads back to the car. After several minutes, they both open the car doors and get inside. Bursting with laughter, Mitch can't contain himself. "Holy shit, man! That was fuckin' crazy. I felt like I was in a Tim Burton movie. I swear, your uncle could be the main character of his next film."

Jacob fastens his seatbelt and takes a deep breath. He looks Mitch in the eyes. "I had to get out of there, Dude, and it wasn't just because his fart smelled like broccoli."

"Why, what happened? Oh, and why the hell were you kicking me? My legs *still* hurt." Mitch doesn't hide his genuine confusion before he starts the car.

After cranking up the air conditioning, Jacob explains, "It's wild, man. So that "idea" my uncle was talking about, that sports drink bottle? Well, that entire meeting actually happened. Now, I don't know if the part about my dad stealing his idea is true…but my dad has been working on that product for the last two years. The freezer in the garage is filled with his prototypes. He just got the patent on it about six months ago."

"Are you kidding me?" Mitch asks.

Jacob's shoulders tighten and he forces a laugh. "No! The freakin' patent certificate is hanging on the wall in his office. The hard part is I have to play dumb every time my uncle brings it up—like I don't know what he's talking about. Here's the kicker: I think my father already has a few purchase orders…and it might even be featured on Home Shopping Network."

"That's so awesome. Is your dad going to give him his quarter every time he sells a unit? Has he told your uncle about this possible Home Shopping Network deal?" Mitch is enthralled by the conversation.

Jacob becomes agitated by the interrogation. "What is this, 20 questions? He isn't going to tell him shit…nada…nothing."

"He said he knows your dad is selling thousands." Mitch continues to push for answers.

"I love my uncle, but even I have to admit sometimes he is an idiot. He doesn't know what the hell he is talking about. I'm sure my grandmother mentioned something to him and he started to conjure up his own version of reality in his mind. They're not even *technically* in stores yet. So, he can't sell any until that happens. Listen, if my dad knew Uncle O had any idea, he would be livid!" Jacob gnaws on his fingernails as he considers the future.

Mitch continues, "I totally forgot to ask. So…what is the name of this *revolutionary* invention?"

Jacob imitates a game show host, "I'm glad you asked! It's called…the Cool-It Sports Drink Bottle." He turns up the radio. "Let's just kill this conversation and get out of here. I need to figure out how I'm going to get Christine's number again."

Mitch shakes his head and is lost in thought as he drives away.

That day will be embedded in my mind forever. Even though trips to my uncle's house were like visiting the circus, there was usually something fascinating that would take place. An unimaginable story, his latest idea…there was never a dull moment. However, the burning question I had to get an answer to was: what did my uncle and father discuss on that day back in 1987? Did my uncle and dad really make a "handshake agreement" that my father never honored? Was that one of the reasons there was such a deep-seated hatred between them? I had always held my father in high regard…believed he was a man of integrity. Was that going to change? I had a plethora of questions and I was going to figure out a way to get them all answered. There was a monumental event coming up in my life and it was only five days away. I knew that there was one person who knew the answers to all my questions and she would be there.

Chapter Four

A Magical Day

• Jacob's 18th birthday •

There is a rapid-fire knock on Jacob's bedroom door. Without warning, the door flings open and Howard tugs the window blinds open. "Get up, Jake-man! Today's the big day, pal. Don't sleep the day away."

Opening one eye, Jacob sees the blurry image of his father standing next to his bed. He is wearing pleated khaki pants and a tucked-in polo shirt with dress shoes.

Jacob's warm drool saturates a large spot on the pillow. "What time is it, Dad?" He pulls the covers over his head and rolls over to the opposite side of his bed.

"It's late. It's eight o'clock…and it's your birthday." Howard mumbles as he pulls out several pieces of corned beef from the deli bag in his hand, and he devours them. He then attempts to sing a doo-wop rendition of the "Happy Birthday" song.

Amused by his father's shenanigans, Jacob stretches like a cat. At the tail end of a yawn, he responds, "OK, big guy. If that song is my birthday gift, please return it." All of a sudden, Jacob feels a thump on his back. He turns over in his bed, still wrapped up in his NBA logo blanket.

"Whose keys are those? Oh, wait…you leased a new car and you're letting me take it out for my birthday?" Jacob teases and winks at his father.

Howard rises up and down on his tippy-toes. "Yeah, something like that. Hustle up and get dressed. I wanna show you something. Meet me outside…with the keys."

Just as Jacob gets out of bed, his telephone rings. Shuffling over to his desk, he grabs the cordless receiver, and in a deep, groggy voice, he answers, "Hello."

"Happy Birthday, my man! Holy shit, you're *officially* 18 years old. I can't believe it!" Mitch shouts into the phone.

Jacob corrects through another yawn, "Well…*technically* I'm still 17 until 10:38 a.m. So, don't rush my life away."

"Listen, I have *the best* birthday present anyone could give you! I'm telling you, man. You won't fuckin' believe it." Mitch can't contain his excitement.

Jacob starts guessing, "Floor seats for the Nets/Bulls game? Please tell me that's what it is. I hate to admit it, but I wanna see MJ drop 50 points on us."

"Dude…it's better than that. I'm talking epic surprise here." Mitch continues to hype up the mystery present. Jacob's anticipation is rising by the second.

"Well, what the hell is it?" He begins to pace back and forth.

"Listen, I'll be over in a little bit. My mom is making me help pick out an outfit for her date tonight. I am sick just thinking about it, but she really likes this guy. Anyway, I will fill you in about my surprise gift once I get to your house," Mitch explains. "Oh, really quick, what time is your party again?"

"Well, everyone will be here around noon, but you can come over whenever you want. By the way, my dad is bringing in a full spread from Bagel Land. I told him to bring home a *massive* bag of the assorted mini muffins." Jacob can't wait to devour his favorite snack.

"Sweet! Looking forward to it. I'll see you soon." In an uncharacteristic show of emotion, Mitch adds, "Listen, I hope this year is a great one. You deserve it. Happy Birthday."

"Thanks, bro. I appreciate that." Jacob hangs up the phone, gets dressed, and grabs the car keys from his bed. He hurries outside. Before he even opens the front door, Jacob hears his father talking to someone on his new mobile phone. Howard is pacing back and forth in the street. He fist-pumps high into the air and cheers.

Jacob walks outside to see a brand-new 1993 Pontiac Bonneville parked in the driveway. It looks like it was driven right off the showroom floor. The sun's bright rays are flickering off the polished, metallic, aqua-blue paint.

The exhilaration in Howard's voice reverberates throughout the street. "That's great news, Stan! This is just the beginning. It's gonna be huge. Talk to you later, pal." Putting his phone back in his pants pocket, he shouts, "Jakey come here!"

"What's going on? Why are there four cars in the driveway?" Jacob lets out a gasp as he circles the Pontiac. He admires the polished chrome rims and futuristic-looking spoiler.

Howard gives an unexpected update: "Well, for starters your Cougar was *just* sold this morning to the Hirsches down the street. Remember "little" Cory? Well, he turned 16 last month and they needed a car for him to get to work."

"What are you talking about? I'm confused. Why would you sell my car, Dad?"

Howard grins and hands Jacob an envelope. Ecstatic, he urges, "Open it, bud." Jacob tears open the envelope with anticipation. He pulls out a letter and reads it to himself.

Jacob,

We have always wanted the best for you. You're filled with compassion and love for people. That is special. You have accomplished a great deal in a short time. Your Bar Mitzvah, graduating high school, and now starting college. Your mom and I are behind you 100%. You have the potential to accomplish great things in your life.

When I was your age, I didn't have all the answers but I knew I had to set a direction and stick to it. You are doing the same thing. I am also proud of you for knowing right from wrong. I can trust that you are responsible. That is important. I know you will work hard and graduate college. Then the world will open up. I know you can do it! Keep being kind to people. It will bring you great joy and happiness.

Happy Birthday. We love you,

Dad & Mom

"Wow, Dad. That's really nice. What got into you? You're never this emotional." Jacob notices something else inside the envelope. He pulls out a check signed by his father. Jacob stumbles backwards and shouts, "Holy shit! A check for $1,500? Are you kidding me?"

Darting at Jacob with his arms open, Howard embraces his son with a loving bear hug. "That's just a little birthday gift from the Hirsches," Howard informs as he playfully pokes Jacob in his stomach.

Immense appreciation radiates from Jacob's smile. "Wow, thanks, Dad. This is a lot of money. I'll deposit it into my savings account on Monday."

"You always seem to make the right decisions. Even when others your age would do the opposite. That's why I gave it to you. You're a good man, Jake." Howard shows his tender side.

Jacob returns the compliment. "I learned about making good life decisions from you." He slides the check into his pocket. "Well…I guess *most* of your decisions are good ones."

"What does that mean?" Howard's taken aback by the subtle insult.

Jacob stares at his father with sad eyes. "Never mind. I don't know what I'm saying. I'm still tired. So, anyway, it's awesome that you gave me this check, but what am I going to cruise around in now that Cory Hirsch will be driving my car?"

"Why don't you take that sweet Pontiac parked over there for a test spin? If you like her, then she's yours," Howard smirks.

Jacob rubs his hands together and leaps into the air. "No test drive needed. I don't like her…I fuckin' love her!"

"Whoa! Keep it down, bud! Just because you're 18 years old now, don't think you're going to start swearing. Got it?" Howard dashes over and opens the door to Jacob's new car like a chauffeur.

Jacob hugs his father. "Thank you, Dad. This means a lot to me. You know I would have been happy with anything you bought me." Jacob's eyes light up as he inhales the new car smell. "I have to ask, what made you decide to buy me such a nice ride? The Cougar still had a lot of life left in her."

Howard can't wait to share the good news. "I haven't spoken to you much about the new product I launched. I need you to *please* act surprised when I tell this to your mother. I just got off the phone with my business partner, Stan Abrams. Walmart just placed a purchase order for...one hundred and fifty thousand units! My Cool-It Sports Drink Bottle will be in 1,600 stores! Listen to this: I spoke to their Senior VP of marketing yesterday. If we meet our sales plan, then we get a display and dedicated endcap in every single store. They are in love with this product!" Howard shimmies in celebration of the news.

"Holy shit, Dad! That's unbelievable! Congratulations. I'm really proud of you." Jacob is fascinated by his father's passion. He recalls the first time he laid eyes on the handmade prototype stored in the garage freezer.

"Let's just say that buying the new car for you was my gift to me. It made me feel good to do it. How about we leave it at that?" Howard beams with pride. Just as Jacob decides to sit down inside his new beauty, he hears a series of rapid car honks from behind him.

"There's the hunky birthday boy!" Mitch shouts from his open car window.

Jacob looks up, thrilled to see his friend. "What's going on, man?"

"I'm good." He pops open the trunk. "How are you doing, Mr. Roth?" Mitch yells as he exits his car and approaches Jacob and his father.

Howard extends an enthusiastic welcome: "What's going on Mr. Mitchell? How is your mom? I haven't seen her since the divorce was made official."

"She's doing good. Tonight, she has a date. It's a little weird, but at least she is getting out onto the dating scene, finally. I know she wants to meet someone." Mitch glances over at the new car.

Howard offers, "Well, if tonight doesn't work out, I can introduce her to my new business partner, Stanley. He's a hell of a nice guy and owns about *twenty* different companies. A real entrepreneur...and a mensch."

"Um, ok...I'll let her know. Thanks!" Mitch gives Howard a thumbs up and then looks at Jacob, expecting some recognition of how awkward that was.

As Howard walks back toward the house, he shouts to Jacob, "I'm leaving soon to go get the food for your party. I told them to give me every type of bagel and salad they have. We're going to have a feast."

"Wait, a minute. Salad?" Jacob is baffled.

Howard the "brunch connoisseur" explains, "Yeah, egg salad, tuna salad, chicken salad, whitefish salad...you know, your salads. You can't *truly* maximize a bagel without them. Oh, I forgot to remind you, my brother is bringing Grandma to the party, but you will need to drive her home later. He has to leave early. Got it?" Howard didn't wait for an answer before going inside.

"Uh, yeah, I got it, Dad." Jacob is pissed that he inherited "drop off duty."

Mitch erupts with exhilaration. "Dude, I have the "gift of all gifts" for you! You won't believe what I'm going to tell you..." He pauses mid-sentence. "Why do you look so down?"

Still in awe, Jacob shakes his head. "It has been a *crazy* morning so far. I don't even know where to begin. First off, I got a new car and a check for $1,500 from my parents."

"Holy shit, man! I was wondering who the hell owned that sweet ride. I had no idea it was your birthday present. It's freakin' beautiful. Did your dad win the lottery or something?" Mitch inspects the new car like it's Kit from Night Rider.

Jacob hesitates. "Dude, he basically did. Remember the sports drink bottle debacle at my uncle's last week?"

"Yeah, I remember. I'm confused. What are you trying to tell me?" Mitch is impatient for the full story.

Leaning against the side of his shimmering Bonneville, Jacob takes a deep breath. "My dad is going to make *a lot* of money."

"Ok, so why do you look depressed as you're telling me that? Come on, cut to the chase." Mitch positions himself next to Jacob and imitates his grandmother's voice. "You're making me meshuga over here. I can't take it."

Jacob lowers his head. "The sports drink bottle…he just got an order for one hundred and fifty thousand units. It's going to be in 1,600 Walmart stores. I don't know what I'm going to do."

Mitch is becoming frustrated. "Jake, please tell me what the heck you're talking about. Why is this bad news? I am literally *beyond* confused right now."

Now standing away from his car, Jacob begins pacing back and forth with his hands in his pockets. "I've had this feeling in my gut. Like I know something isn't right. I'm telling you, Mitch, I really think there is some truth to what my uncle told us. You know, about my dad stealing his idea. I gotta get some answers and find out where that idea came from."

"Calm down—it's your birthday, for God's sake. You're all flustered and schvitzing like crazy. Relax!" Mitch walks over and playfully massages Jacob's shoulders.

Taking a deep breath to focus his thoughts, Jacob agrees. "You're right, man. I need to just enjoy the day. So, tell me what is this *incredible* gift you were talking about. I can't imagine what it could be."

"Holy shit! You totally distracted me when you started crying about your dad becoming rich. You're gonna owe me for the rest of your life when I tell you this," Mitch brags as he flexes his biceps like he was Hulk Hogan.

Jacob shakes Mitch's shoulders. "What is it, man? Tell me already? This better be good."

"So, yesterday my mom asked me if I got you a birthday card. I'm like, Mom, it's his 18th birthday party. We don't give cards to each other anymore. Anyway, she didn't shut up about it, so I ran into ShopRite to get you one. It's in the car, by the way," Mitch explains.

Thrusting his arms into the air, chuckling, Jacob begs, "For God's sake, man…get to the fuckin' point already…Please!"

"Sorry, it's my ADHD. I didn't take my medication today. OK, so I'm picking out a card for you and I hear someone say my name. I look up and it's freakin' Christine!"

Jacob shouts, "Shut the hell up, man!" as he begins to nervously bite his nails.

"Tell me about it. I couldn't believe this was happening. It gets better. She then proceeds to ask me where *you* are and why *you* haven't called her." Mitch can hardly contain his excitement. He does his best Arsenio Hall "fist pump."

Jacob is desperate to hear more. In a frenzy, he high-fives Mitch like they were tag team partners in a wrestling match.

"Relax, it gets even better…I promise. So, I got a little verklempt and told her that you left the napkin with her number on it at the restaurant. Don't kill me." Mitch puts up his hands as a shield.

Jacob shakes his head in utter embarrassment. "Come on, man! You told her that?"

"Sorry, but I felt like I was under a ton of pressure. By the way, she looked ab-so-lutely incredible. She must have just come from the tanning salon. I believe she was wearing my favorite perfume…Sunflowers. Wait, let me stay focused here. The next thing I know she's asking me what you and I are doing Saturday. Of course, I told her right away it was your birthday party," Mitch explains the encounter with detailed precision.

Pretending to cry, Jacob responds, "Oh my God, Dude! You freakin' told her I was having a *birthday party* while you were holding my *birthday card* in your hand?"

"It gets a little worse before it gets better…but it does get better," Mitch confirms.

Jacob takes a deep breath and then exhales. He grumbles, "What happened?"

"Your dad asked me to buy party hats and party blowers. I was also holding those when she walked up," Mitch confesses as he gradually backs away.

"Well, why didn't you just tell her I was having my birthday party at Chuck E. Cheese and that my theme was Teenage Mutant Ninja Turtles?"

Mitch grins at Jacob and remains silent. After several agonizing seconds he then confirms, "No, I didn't say that. Come on give me a little credit."

Jacob snickers. "With you, I never know, man. I don't put *anything* past you. Keep going. What happened next?"

Mitch's smile signals that he is ready to reveal the big news. "I invited her to your party and she said she would stop by!" Proud of himself, he executes a flawless version of the Macarena.

Jacob falls to his knees and shouts, "You gotta be kidding me! Holy shit, that's awesome. I wonder if she is going to actually show up."

"Why wouldn't she? When I invited her, she gave me the biggest smile and said, 'Sure, I'd love to stop by.'" Mitch imitates a girl's voice.

Jacob jumps up, embraces Mitch, and lifts him off of the ground. "OK, put me down. You're gonna break my back. Hang on, I have something for us." Mitch hustles over to his car and opens the trunk. He returns holding two canned beers and tosses one to Jacob. The boys fist bump and commemorate the historic occasion with a toast.

"Here's to turning 18 and your future wife stopping by to help celebrate," Mitch broadcasts to the entire street as he holds up his beer.

Jacob replies, "Thanks, bro. Here's to my family not embarrassing the crap out of me *if* she actually does stop by." Taking a sip of beer, Jacob immediately spits the sour liquid onto the driveway. "That tastes like warm piss, man. What did you bring me, the ShopRite brand?"

"I snagged them from my refrigerator yesterday and hid them in my car. I think they were from my mom's New Year's Eve party from three years ago." Mitch scrunches his face as he turns the can upside down and pours the beer onto Jacob's driveway.

Without warning, Howard flings open the front door and dashes outside. Jacob hides his beer can underneath the car. Mitch slides his inside the waist band of his shorts.

"Do you guys wanna come with me to pick up the food? I'm heading over now to get everything," Howard announces as he points his nose into the air, wrinkles his upper lip and begins to make an exaggerated sniffing noise. The boys look at each other, stone-faced.

Howard expresses his disgust and shouts, "Why does it smell like piss out here now? Did someone take a leak on my driveway?"

"Oh, that. Yeah, the Lipman's dog just ran over and peed on our driveway and then bolted away," Jacob answers, unable to hide his guilty grin.

Howard vents, "That damn furball better stay off our property. Next time spray it with a hose. I mean it."

Jacob responds, "Yeah, I'll keep a look-out, big guy. That little white furball is vicious."

Howard zips over to his car, gets in, and shouts through the open window, "I'll be back in a little bit. Uncle Dan called, and he's stopping by with your Grandma Audrey in an hour. Make sure you spend some time talking to her when she gets here."

"Oh, don't worry, I will. I have *a lot* of catching up to do with her," Jacob winks at Mitch. After backing out of the driveway, Howard gives two goodbye honks and speeds away.

While scratching his head, Mitch asks Jacob, "Are you going to ask your grandma about who really invented that sports drink bottle?"

"It's not the sports bottle that was the invention. The patent was on the blue ice cartridge that hangs down from *inside* the bottle. My dad owns that. I was reading up on patents and that type of stuff. People can make millions of dollars off of the smallest enhancements to products. A slight change of something can warrant a patent being issued," Jacob clarifies.

Mitch is captivated by the situation. "Wow, that's crazy. So basically, even if Uncle O gave your dad the idea for this blue ice cartridge, unless he is listed on the patent certification, he won't see a penny."

"You are correct. Even if he "presented" the idea to my dad, and let's say they actually shook hands on it, unless there is a legal agreement, he will never see one red cent." Jacob paces and runs his fingers through his hair.

"It's nice of you to try and help your uncle, but I think you should stay out of everything. Let your dad make a ton of money and just be happy. Look, you already got a new car out of it. Shit, maybe he will buy you a house when you graduate. Why would you risk screwing all that up?" Mitch questions.

Placing both of his hands onto Mitch's shoulders, Jacob looks him directly in the eyes.

"'Cause it's the right thing to do. That's why. Let's go inside and get a snack."

I remember the confused expression on Mitch's face when I gave him that answer. He was absolutely shocked that I would be willing to risk the opportunity to receive "material things" by doing the right thing. I knew my uncle and father never got along. The stories that were told to me saddened my heart. I always wondered what it would be like to have a brother, so the fact that my dad had one that he treated like shit really upset me. In a way, Mitch and I looked at my uncle like an older brother. Mitch wouldn't admit it, but he also had a soft spot for Uncle O. I guess it was because his brother passed away. Not having a sibling was really tough for us both. We had each other, though, and it was a bond that would be a forever friendship.

An hour later, the doorbell rings. "Jake, go get the door!" Howard shouts from his office.

"I'm coming. Hang on!" Jacob yells as he speed walks toward the front door and opens it. There is a petite, older woman, holding a medium-size Louis Vuitton handbag. She has on oversized glasses with protective sun lenses clipped on the front. Her puffy, shoulder-length, silver hair is set perfectly in place. As she opens her handbag to take a birthday card out, Jacob welcomes her with joy. "Hi, Grandma. How are you? Come on inside. It's so good to see you."

Taking her arm, Jacob escorts his grandmother inside the house. He leads her to the couch in the family room where they both sit down.

"Where's Uncle Dan?" Jacob asks as he takes his grandmother's handbag and sets it to the side.

Oh, he walked me up to the door and said he had to go. He wanted me to tell you Happy Birthday, sweetheart." Jacob's grandmother caresses his arm.

I never understood why my dad thought so highly of Uncle Dan. He was the biggest dick I knew. Blowing off my 18th birthday and leaving his 76-year-old mother at the door by herself was typical of him. He was divorced two times and the "family rumor" was that he cheated on both of his wives. His three kids had almost nothing to do with him because there was an abusive side that lurked underneath his snake-oil-salesman persona.

Then you have Uncle O, who always just wanted my dad's love and respect, but he never got it. It didn't make sense and I don't fully understand it to this day.

"Honey, here's your birthday card. There's a little check in there for you to use however you would like. I just can't believe that you're 18 years old today. It seems like just yesterday was your Bar Mitzvah," Jacob's grandmother reminisces.

He leans into his grandmother and kisses her on the forehead. "Thank you, Grandma. I really appreciate that. I'll probably save the money for now. Dad set up a checking account for me. How is Uncle O? I really wish he could have come today."

Softly placing her hand under Jacob's chin, Audrey looks her grandson in the eyes. "You're such a sweet young man, Jacob. Your heart overflows with kindness. The love you have for your uncle is very special. He hasn't had an easy life, you know. From the time he was in grade school, he really struggled with his learning disability. He would get frustrated because learning came so easy to your father and your Uncle Dan. I know he didn't mean to, but many times he would act out in anger and resentment toward his older brothers. Sometimes it would even get physical. After your grandfather passed away, your uncle started to get even more depressed. You know, it's never easy losing a parent, but it is even more difficult when you're only 14 years old. Your grandfather and uncle were the best of friends. They did *everything* together. The bond they had was really unbreakable, you know. It was unlike anything I have ever seen." Audrey closes her eyes. "When your grandfather died so did a part of your uncle."

Jacob takes his grandmother's trembling hand and holds it. Her lashes flutter as she pushes away the tears welling in her eyes.

"Grandma, if this is too hard to speak about, we can stop. I don't want you to get upset." Jacob contemplates whether he should change the subject of the conversation.

She smiles. "It's important that you know the truth, my darling grandson. Especially now that you are old enough to *really* understand it. I remember the day your father and uncle got into a terrible argument over something silly. It may have been about what they were watching on television. Your father would always call your uncle dumb or stupid. But this day would be the last time. Before I knew it, they were actually fist-fighting like enemies who despised each other. It was so bad that I had to call the police, Jacob. Your uncle was much bigger than your father, and still is today. After years of being teased and the trauma of losing his father, your uncle just snapped. He hit your father so hard that he broke his nose and fractured two of his ribs. Howard had to go to the hospital and was there for two days."

Jacob's mouth drops open and his eyes widen. Hearing the violent details stirs his emotions. "That's *really* sad, Grandma. Uncle O is a good person. I mean that was wrong of him to do, it really was. That's terrible to hear, but why wouldn't my dad just love him back? I know that's all Uncle O ever wanted."

"Oh, sweetie, I have asked myself that same question many, many times. It took me years to figure out the answer. Your father didn't love himself back then. So, it wasn't possible for him to love someone else. Even his own brother." Jacob's grandmother takes out her handkerchief and gently pats the tears off her face.

Jacob's head hangs low and he remains quiet. He uses the collar of his shirt to wipe his eyes. Placing her arm around her grandson, Audrey asks, "Does that help you understand why your uncle and father have such deep anger toward each other? As their mother, it makes me very sad. I hope and pray every night that one day their relationship will be repaired."

"I do, too. Grandma, I know when I go over to see Uncle O, a lot of the stories he tells me aren't true. But I always feel like at least a small part is." Jacob grins.

She pats Jacob's knee. "He is a great storyteller and always will be. Just like your grandfather—anything to get a rise out of someone. Your uncle loves to take a boring story and make it sound more thrilling. You know, he really should have been an author."

Locking eyes with his grandmother, Jacob looks around and leans in. "Or an inventor?"

"Oh, honey, I think we should probably end this discussion. Won't the guests be arriving soon for your party?" Audrey asks with an awkward pause. She attempts to stand up and falls back into the deep sofa cushions.

"Grandma, tell me about my father's new product, the Cool-It. The one with the blue ice cartridge that hangs from the top of the sports drink bottle. What do you know about it?" Fidgeting, Jacob crosses and uncrosses his legs.

Taken aback, Audrey responds, "Not too much. I know he told me Walmart will be carrying it in many of their stores. Other than that, I don't know that much about your father's business affairs."

Jacob presses for more info. "I need you to please tell me what you know. Whose idea was it to create that hanging blue ice cartridge? The part of the product that my dad got a patent for."

"Whooo, had I known this was going to be such an emotional visit I would have rested up more before coming over." Audrey becomes visibly shaken.

Jacob responds with genuine remorse. "I'm sorry, Grandma. Believe me. I am not trying to upset you. I just need to know if Uncle O invented it or not. My dad signed a purchase order for one hundred and fifty thousand units. I need to know if Uncle O is entitled to a part of the profits."

"Honey, your uncle is fine. You know I give him money each month to pay his bills and buy groceries. He has everything he needs. There's no reason for you to worry about anything." Audrey reaches inside her purse for her compact. Looking in the mirror, she pats her hair back into place.

Jacob ratchets up the tension. "I need to know the truth, Grandma. This isn't about the money. This is about my father's integrity and doing the right thing. If Uncle O gave my father the idea in exchange for part of the profits one day, then that's what he should get."

"I admire you so much, I really do. Your grandfather would have been so proud of the way you have embraced your uncle over the years. Other than me, you are really the only other person who sees the good in his soul. I will always love you for that." She leans back and sighs. "Something inside of me believes that one day many people will see the same thing we do. I know it will happen." Taking a moment to compose her thoughts, Audrey continues. "Ok, honey, let me *finally* answer the question you asked me."

All of a sudden, Howard yanks open his office door and zooms out. He blasts into the family room like the road runner.

"Damn it," Jacob grumbles to himself.

Howard apologizes by shouting, "Sorry, I couldn't get off the phone. I had an important call. What's going on, Mom? I got some *incredible* news! This day keeps getting better. Where's Dan? I thought he was staying for a while."

Jacob is heated. "Yeah, good ole Uncle Dan, dropped Grandma off at the front door like a UPS package and left. I never saw the dickhead."

"Hey, don't be disrespectful, Jakester! Not cool at all, especially in front of your grandmother. Don't let me hear that type of language again. I know he had an important business meeting he had to attend." Howard attempts to justify his brother's behavior.

Jacob's grandmother changes the subject. "So, Howard, tell us, what is the *incredible* news? Also, can someone please pull me off this couch before it swallows me up?"

"Everyone, fasten your seat belt. I am getting close to landing a deal with Home Shopping Network. I could be going live with the Cool-It on *three* different shows! Can you believe this? This "side hustle" is turning out to be something huge!" Howard pulls his mother up off the couch.

Strolling into the room, Mitch gives a shout-out, "Congrats, Mr. Roth. Wow, that's amazing news! Maybe Jacob can be on television doing the demonstration."

"That's not a bad idea, Mitch. What do you think, Jake? We can throw a Cool-It embroidered polo shirt on you. Then have you on set sitting next to me as we sell the hottest product of 1993. Some father-son bonding time," Howard suggests as he pats Jacob on his back.

Jacob's courtesy laugh disguises his uneasiness. "I'm good, Dad, but thanks for the offer. Congrats! That's exciting news. I'm happy for you."

Thanks, buddy. Listen, I'm going to start setting up for the party soon. Mitch, do you have the party favors I asked you to pick up?" Howard bounces from foot to foot.

Jacob interrupts, "Oh, yeah, Dad, about that. Can we please skip the party hats and party blowers this year? There's a girl stopping by who I am friends with. I kind of want to keep my party low key, if you know what I mean."

"A girl? What's her name?" Jacob's mother inquires from the next room.

Howard's ecstatic. "That's fabulous news, Jake-man! I can't wait to meet her. I'll make sure my video camera is charged and ready to go. Lucky for you I *just* bought a 6-pack of blank cassettes. I'm ready to roll."

"WHOA! Relax everyone. Mom, her name is Christine. Dad, you are *not* videotaping her! Got it? Please don't embarrass me. I'm *begging* you." Jacob places his palms together as if he is praying.

So far, my birthday was turning out to be an emotional rollercoaster. Unfortunately, my plan to get the truth from my grandmother fell short by about two minutes. My father was the type of person who got shit done, there is no doubt about that. At the same time, he would "bend" the truth if it meant getting to the finish line. As I got older there were several times I caught him red-handed in a white lie. He would always sidestep his way out of it, but I knew what was going on. Here's the thing: there was only one person he never would bullshit...never lie to...and that was his own mother.

I will never forget the look on my grandmother's face when I asked her the question that was weighing heavy on my heart. I could see the truth buzzing in her eyes. I got the feeling she knew exactly what happened on October 27, 1987. Eventually, I would have to confront my father about that day. It was something I was not looking forward to.

When the doorbell rings, Jacob's nerves begin to pulsate through his body. He directs everyone into the family room so he can open the door in privacy. Through the etched, frosted glass window on the front door, he can see the blurry image of a teenage girl. Perspiration begins to slicken the palms of his hands. Jacob takes several quick breaths and wipes his palms on his shorts. He braces for impact.

"Hey, how are you? Mitch told me you may stop by today. Come on in." Jacob massages the back of his neck and greets his guest with a gawky smile.

Upon entering the house, Christine attempts to hug Jacob at the same exact time he tries to shake her hand. "Oh, whoops...sorry!" Jacob mumbles as he puts his sweaty hand down. The awkward hug adds to his discomfort.

Giggling and oblivious to the clumsy hello, she responds, "Well, Happy Birthday! Oh my God. I can't believe you are 18 today. It totally feels like we just graduated from middle school. Here, I got you a little something." Christine hands Jacob a gift bag with colorful tissue paper poking out of the top.

Jacob fights to keep his hand from shaking. "That is really nice. You didn't have to do that. Just showing up to my party is good enough. Come inside, I'll introduce you to my family. My dad just picked up brunch from Bagel Land. I think you like their food, right?"

Christine can sense his uneasiness. "Are you OK? You seem a little stressed out. And, yes, I love their food. Especially their mini muffins." She smiles at Jacob.

Despite realizing he was sweating, Jacob reassures, "I'm totally fine. I couldn't be more relaxed."

She runs her hand through her hair and steels herself to say, "You know something…I've always thought you had really pretty eyes. They say *a lot* about you."

Jacob is spellbound and struggles to utter the words, "Thank you."

Like a group of New York City tourists led by Howard, everyone flocks toward the front door. They are all wearing party hats and holding party blowers as they approach Christine.

Howard announces, "Come on in! The birthday party is ready to start. Grab a bagel and sit down with us. We are so excited that you're here."

Mortified, Jacob whispers to Christine, "I'm going to apologize in advance for what's about to happen. Please don't hold it against me."

She is flattered by the attention and whispers into his ear, "I'm just happy to be here to celebrate with you."

I'm sure you could predict how the rest of my birthday party went. Between my father singing "Happy Birthday, Mr. Jakester" and my mother making me wear a party hat, it was quite a memorable day. Mitch was right: having Christine there was definitely the best birthday gift I had ever gotten. I didn't know what would come of it, but for the first time I started to actually believe that perhaps she did like me. That night I couldn't stop thinking about her captivating smile. Each time she looked at me that day, it was as if time stood still and I could see a future with her. It was almost too good to be true. Things were falling into place with ease. I also knew I had to play it cool and not scare her away.

It was a great birthday, but finding out the truth about the Cool-It was still top of my mind. I didn't want to jump the gun, but something in my gut told me my uncle's accusations were true. He didn't have many friends, so I knew tracking down someone I could "politely" interrogate would not be easy. From my grandmother's reaction I could tell there was way more to this story. I wasn't going to let up until I found out the answer.

Chapter Five

Bagels for Ostaf

• July 31, 1993 •

T he telephone rings and startles Jacob, who is abruptly awakened from a deep sleep. His eyelids are closed as he reaches onto his nightstand, fumbling around for the cordless phone. In an irritated and groggy voice, he mumbles, "Hello? Who is this?"

Speaking with a warm, vibrant tone, the female caller asks, "Are you going to sleep the day away, silly?"

Rising to attention, Jacob stutters with embarrassment, "Uh, hey, um, how are you doing? I'm so sorry. I totally thought you were Mitch. My caller ID isn't working. I need to change the batteries."

Christine does her best impersonation and imitates Jacob. "Well, I'd hate to be him, having to listen to that *deep, grumpy, morning voice.*"

Jacob snickers and sets the record straight. "Well, just so you know, you can call me any time and I promise: no grumpy voice."

"I'll hold you to that. So, today's the big day. You ready for it?" Christine asks with genuine interest.

Doubt begins to creep in. "Well, the real question is…are *you* ready for it?" Jacob slides out of bed and walks over to his closet.

"I was born ready, baby!" Christine jokes. "Now come over and pick me up so we can get our day going. A part of me is really looking forward to this. Leave now, OK?"

Jacob smirks. "I'll be at your house in 20 minutes. Oh, and make sure you bring a pair of nose plugs."

"Ok, now you're starting to scare me." Christine's reservations were well founded.

Jacob reassures her, "You'll be all right. I promise. It's going to be an experience you won't ever forget. I'll see you in a little bit."

"Hurry up. Bye!" Christine shouts.

Jacob gets dressed and rummages through his closet shelves. He slides over three shoe boxes that are full of Nintendo game cartridges. Reaching onto the top shelf, he grabs a small cardboard carton. It's taped closed. On the way out of his room, Jacob picks up an envelope on his dresser and slides it into his pocket. He grabs his backpack and throws it over his shoulder. In stealth mode, he tiptoes through the house, clenching the carton. Hoping he goes unnoticed, Jacob speed walks the last 10 feet to the front door. His hand is steady as he grasps the lock. Just as he begins to turn the latch, he hears his parents' bedroom door creak open. Praying it's not his father, he looks away.

"You don't even tell us you're leaving, sweetie? What's in the box?" Jacob's mother, Linda, probes.

Relieved, Jacob breathes lighter. "Hey, Mom. Sorry, I didn't want to disturb you guys." He places the mystery box onto the floor.

Walking over to the couch, Linda requests, "Come sit down for a few minutes with me, sweetie. I want to talk to you."

Jacob obliges. Apprehensive, he asks, "What's going on, Mom? I'm running late. Why do you need to talk to me?"

"Well, first off, I *really* like Christine. She seems like a very sweet girl. Her smile tells a lot about her. It's sincere and genuine… just like you are, Jake." Linda takes his hand and holds it. The tension tightens as the crescendo builds.

Jacob glances away and rolls his eyes. "Um, thanks, Mom. She's a good person. It's nothing serious, we have only gone out a few times."

"I saw how she looked at you the day of your party. It was with admiration. Almost like she knows the kindness that exists inside of you," Linda compliments.

Weary, Jacob continues the charades. "Thanks, Mom. That's nice of you to say. I do my best. I'm not perfect."

"No one is perfect, but the way you care about people, especially your uncle, is commendable. I'm sorry that your father and I don't feel the same way about him that you do. We have our reasons." Linda ignites the fuse. Her disdain for Ostaf lurks behind her sneer.

Jacob struggles to contain his frustration. "You just act that way toward him because of Dad. Of course, Uncle O isn't perfect. Just like Dad isn't either. I really don't understand how someone can treat their own flesh and blood with so much hatred. It's terrible. I believe with all my heart that Uncle O just wants Dad to be proud of him. That's all! Something so damn simple."

"It's *never* going to happen, Jacob. Your uncle was awful to your father when they were younger. Not only was he verbally abusive to your father, he was also that way to your grandmother. You love your grandmother…don't you?"

Jacob is seething. He can't hide his annoyance and his voice begins to shake. "Are you kidding me, Mom? Really? That's the road you want to go down? I know the entire story. Grandma understands why Uncle O was that way when he was younger. Clearly you don't. He hasn't had an easy life."

"I just don't like to see my kind-hearted son being taken advantage of." Linda stands up and unleashes a tirade. "And all his stupid inventions are worthless! Not one idea he has ever come up with has amounted to anything. He's a phony and a detriment to this family." She glances at the cardboard box. "Must I remind you about the world-famous "Super Straw"? I mean, who doesn't want to use a six-foot straw to drink their soda? I also remember he tried to get your father to invest money into building a prototype for an engine that used corn syrup instead of gas. He's a fool, Jacob. I wish you would realize that and stop wasting your time with him. In the end, all he is going to do is take what he can from you."

Heartbroken, Jacob snaps back. "Wow. I don't know what to say. I really don't. What the hell does he take from me? Old, dusty cassette tapes and video games that have been rotting in my closet for years. Things I literally haven't used in a decade. The guy has nothing. Why does it bother you if I try and help him out? Not to mention that he hates it when I give him things to sell. It makes him feel bad about himself…And remember, in life, all it takes is one ticket to win the lottery. One idea to change the world."

Jacob's mother responds with palpable sarcasm, "OK, sweetie, as long as you believe your uncle can change the world, that's all that matters." She pats Jacob's hand. "Oh, if you like Christine and don't want to scare her away, please do not bring her anywhere near your uncle."

Jacob stands up, peers at his mother, and fights the urge to argue. At the last moment, he decides to remain quiet as he picks up the box, opens the door, and trudges outside.

Nothing would frustrate me more than when my mother would make her accusations about my uncle. I knew she was just regurgitating the bullshit my father fed her. There was a time when my father could tolerate him enough to let him come into our house. I must have been seven or eight years old, but I remember him driving my parents crazy. They didn't have the patience for his stale jokes, tasteless comments, and general shenanigans. As I got older, I began to realize that before you judge someone, try to have enough self-awareness to hit the pause button. Understand that *most* people have good buried inside them. Even the ones who annoy the shit out of us. Every person has a story and every story molds us into the person we become. I wished that my parents could see the loving spirit of my uncle. It was there, buried beneath the rough and rugged exterior of his being. I could see it. Why couldn't anyone else? It would be years before I would find out the answer to that question.

Jacob walks to his car and kicks a pine cone lying on the ground. He backs out of the driveway, then inserts his CD *Pop Hits of 1983*. As he turns up the volume and lowers the windows, thoughts of his uncle flood his mind. The sweet memories and nostalgic music begin to calm him.

Several minutes later, he pulls into a brick-laid driveway and parks his car. Jacob hurries to ring the bell. The door flies open, and Christine bursts outside to greet him with a warm embrace. She's holding a large, brown paper bag.

The tension lingers and Jacob grins. "Are you *sure* you're ready to meet him? You can change your mind and I won't be upset. I promise."

"I'm ready, silly…and no, I'm not changing my mind. I know how important he is to you. I think it's awesome that you see the good in him. More people in the world should follow your lead." Christine grabs Jacob's hands and pulls him toward the car. "Let's go! It's a beautiful day."

Curious, Jacob asks, "What's in the bag?"

"Breakfast…I ran out to Bagel Land earlier. I picked up bagels, a few salads, and a bunch of mini muffins. They are the best. I can eat them like peanuts." Christine smiles.

Thrown for a loop, Jacob stares at the bag. "Salads?"

"Sure, you gotta have all your salads…tuna salad, chicken salad, and egg salad," Christine explains. They both open the car doors and get inside.

"Jeez, you sound exactly like my dad. He loves his salads…and his bagels. I guess that's the one thing my uncle and father have in common. By the way, my Uncle is going to *love* you for bringing him food." Jacob reveals the secret to Ostaf's affection.

Christine changes the conversation. "So, tell me again: where does your uncle live?"

"Literally, in the boondocks. It's an adventure to get there, so be ready. Remind me to tell you the story about how Mitch almost became fish food the last time we went. It was like a scene out of an *Indiana Jones* movie." Jacob laughs as he recalls the infamous bridge incident.

Christine's demeanor becomes serious. "I feel like I should be wearing a safari outfit. Does he live in a house?"

"Um, technically, yes. My grandmother's cousin, Ida, owned the house back in the early-1970s. After she passed away it sat empty for over a decade before my grandma bought it for my uncle. The story is that Ida was found still sitting in her rocking chair holding her sewing needle years after she died.

"Shut the hell up! You better be kidding," Christine shouts while squeezing Jacob's arm.

He makes the confession, "I'm just teasing you. Relax. It wasn't years after she died. It was just a few months."

"You're such an idiot. Are you trying to freak me out? We haven't even gotten there yet and I need a cigarette. I don't even smoke." Christine jokes as she slaps Jacob's shoulder.

Like an airplane pilot, Jacob makes the official announcement. "Ok, buckle up and hold on tight. We're off to visit the great Ostaf Roth."

Christine spots Jacob's folder of CDs on the side of her seat. She opens it up and skims through the options. Pulling out the Peter Gabriel disk titled, *So*, she erupts, "Oh-my-God! I love this album! *"In Your Eyes"* is my favorite song. I've always imagined dancing to it on my wedding day," she sighs.

"Get out of here! It's my favorite song, too. I *love* the acoustic version." Jacob is amazed by the coincidence.

Christine is reluctant, but divulges her secret. "You know that day at your party. Well, that song was playing in my mind when I looked at you."

"Ok, you're *totally* making me blush now." Jacob squirms as the perspiration begins to dot his forehead. Both of his hands grasp the steering wheel. He takes a gasping breath, smiles, and the voyage to Osaf's chateau begins.

I could not believe that out of the forty CDs I had organized into my storage case she picked the one with my favorite song in the world. We weren't officially dating, but I started to experience feelings I had never had before. It was getting real. You have to understand, I was 18 years old and this was the first girl I really started to care about. I had hung out with a few girls during my high school days, but either I got tired of them or they got tired of me. (Probably always the latter). When I look back, it's hard to believe that even at that young age, I could already see a future with her. I knew I needed Christine to be part of my world. I wasn't quite sure why, but then again sometimes you don't need to know why. Just be your best self and live your life. The waves of time will settle exactly where they should.

Thirty minutes later, Jacob veers onto the secluded dirt road and begins the backwoods expedition to his uncle's house. The car begins to wobble from the large pebbles and rocks covering the desolate one-way path. As Jacob drives over the uneven gravel, Christine grasps his leg. "You weren't kidding. This place is *literally* in the middle of nowhere." She stares at the corroded shells of dated, abandoned machines. Rust-covered farm equipment, refrigerators, and washing machines line the path like estate statues.

Jacob shares the backstory. "People around here know that my uncle is an inventor, so they drop off their old, broken appliances. He strips them to the bone. I mean down to the last screw and bolt. Some parts are used for his next "extraordinary" invention and others he sells. It's like a grave yard out here."

"In an odd, poetic kind of way, it's almost mystical." She glances at the clock. "Are we close to his house yet?" Christine admires the blissful wooded scenery. Two black bear cubs appear in the distance. They're playful and paw each other as they mosey across the path.

"We're getting close. Wow, look over there. I can't believe it. They are so freakin' cute!" Jacob shouts and puts the car in park. He's quick to roll up the windows and turn on the air conditioner.

Christine is awed by the rare encounter. "Oh my God. I love being out of the city! Let's get out and walk closer to them. Maybe if we are quiet, we can get a closer look."

Jacob's warning is blunt. "Not unless you want to be lunch for the mother."

"What do you mean?" Christine pushes her face against the passenger side window, admiring the adorable cubs.

"Momma bear is lurking around here somewhere. She's watching those cubs like a hawk and will maul anyone who attempts to go near them." Jacob locks the car doors.

Christine is enthralled. "How the heck do you know so much about bears?"

"Uncle O told me a crazy story about his friend who snuck up on a group of cubs and tried to pick one of them up. Out of nowhere, the mother chased the guy down like a gazelle. She grabbed him by the waistband of his pants and started to drag him into the woods." Jacob tells the tale as if he is sitting next to a crackling bonfire at a Scouts overnighter.

Christine grips the door handle. "Holy shit! What happened to the guy?"

Jacob leans in and continues to narrate each detail like a seasoned camp counselor. "Uncle O runs after the bear. Now keep in mind, black bears can run up to 35 miles per hour. I would imagine with an adult-size man clenched in her jaws, we are talking half of that speed. Either way, she is running fast. So, my uncle eventually catches up to the scene of the crime. He sprints full speed at the savage bear and tackles her like a WWF wrestler bouncing off the ropes. As he puts the bear into a headlock, she *finally* lets go of his friend. He tussles with her for another few minutes, before the bear springs up and dashes into the woods."

Christine's eyes widen as she fans herself. "Holy shit! That sounds like a story out of a movie."

Jacob can't restrain his boisterous laugh. "Because it is. Even though I love the big guy, he adds on parts of the story that never happened. If you dig deep enough, there is usually a *small* amount of truth mixed in. The rest is just simply made up. That's just one of a hundred stories I could tell you. One day when we're bored, I'll fill you in on the time he snuck onto the set of *American Bandstand* and played the tambourine with KC and The Sunshine Band.

"Wow, it sounds like your uncle should have been a screenplay writer. He seems like a great storyteller. You *totally* had me on the edge of my seat with that bear story," Christine says, as a genuine compliment.

Jacob stares aimlessly through the window. "Yeah, there are a lot of things he would be good at."

Christine attempts to change the conversation. "Well, thanks for saving my life, because my stupid ass probably would have gotten out of the car to try and pet those little guys."

She takes Jacob's hand and gazes deep into his eyes. The sun's golden rays are shining on his face. Placing her hand on Jacob's cheek, she turns his head toward hers. She leans in, closes her eyes, and presses her lips to his. The song "In Your Eyes" repeats in the background.

There is a thundering knock on the driver's side window. Startled, Christine shrieks, as she looks over and sees a man with thick, black-framed glasses, and a unmanicured, scraggly, gray beard. The stranger smirks and waves in a juvenile fashion as he pushes his face against the window.

Unable to hide his embarrassment, Jacob turns toward Christine and whispers into her ear, "I am *so* sorry." Jacob stares at the man as he rolls down the window. "Christine, this is my Uncle O."

"My apologies. I didn't mean to disrupt your make-out session, but someone I know from the flea market is supposed to drop off a vintage 1978 supermarket freezer. The compressors in those things are worth a fortune if they're in good shape." Ostaf clears his throat as he runs his grease-covered fingers through his beard.

Jacob takes a deep breath to ease his angst. "Well, we just drove in and we didn't see anyone. Do you want a lift? There's room in the back seat." Praying that he declines the offer, Christine looks at Ostaf and displays a warmhearted "courtesy" smile.

"Thanks, Dude, but I gotta meet this guy really quick and then I will have him drop me off at the bridge. This compressor could be worth a few hundred bucks if it works. Keep your toes crossed for me. My mom said you weren't coming over until noon. What happened?" Ostaf coughs up phlegm and spits it over the car.

Jacob shakes his head in embarrassment. "We wanted to come over a little early and hang with you. We brought some bagels and a bunch of different salads."

Uncle O scratches his armpit. "Who the hell eats salads with bagels? That's really weird, Dude."

"Ya know, ya salads: egg salad, tuna salad, and chicken salad," Christine answers, doing her best South Jersey waitress impression.

Ostaf's bellowing laugh permeates the air. "You got me! I like her, Jacob." He attempts to high-five Christine through the opened window. With no hesitation, Jacob reaches over and sacrifices his own hand.

"We'll see you back at the house in a little bit, Uncle O." Jacob exhales and closes the window. "I know. *Please* don't hate me." He starts the car and cruises in the direction of the obscured bridge.

Christine cradles her cheeks in both hands and shouts, "WOW! Oh-my-God. You weren't kidding about him. What a character."

"I told you. He is definitely one of a kind. Hopefully you won't want to stop hanging out with me after you have breakfast with him. Oh, and just so you know: he is going to tell you a few things. Just keep giving him the sweet smiles like you did before and you will be fine," instructs Jacob, pleased with how this was going so far.

Christine grins. "You caught that? I hope he didn't think I was being a jerk. I don't want to be on his bad side."

"Don't worry, he was just happy you smiled at him. So, here's the deal. He is going to bring up the following situations. Like I told you earlier, most of his stories have little to no truth to them. Ready? Here they are in no particular order: He is a master inventor and has million-dollar ideas written down on papers in his basement…He doesn't need anything from anyone…He dated a smokin' hot actress…and the last one…He can't stand my father because he stole his idea for an invention," Jacob explains like an attorney preparing his client.

Christine wants more details. "Did the last one you said really happen?"

"I'm not sure. You could say I'm on a mission to try and find out. The crazy thing is the way my uncle tells the story, it would be hard to make it up. My gut tells me it might be true. I need to find out more about this "hot actress" he supposedly dated. Last week he told Mitch and me that she was with him the day he thought of the idea. I'm hoping she may have the information I need. The wild part is my father is getting ready to launch this product. It's going to be big time. I'll tell you all about it later." Jacob parks the car. "Ok, congratulations. We made it to the next level of Jumanji. Here's the bridge we need to cross to get to his house… and again, I use the term "house" loosely," Jacob laughs as he exits the car.

Christine steps out of her side and grabs the bag of food from the back seat. The stream next to them trickles around the rocks and swerves around the masses of trees. The sun's rays shoot through the surrounding branches and leaves, creating breathtaking silhouettes on the ground. Chirping birds communicate with each other through the summer morning air.

Jacob approaches Christine and places his arm around her shoulders. She nestles close to him. In unison, they take a deep breath and bask in the calm of nature. The breeze strengthens and blows through their hair.

"You know, it is beautiful out here. So relaxing. It's just…peaceful." Christine is awed by the picturesque rural landscape.

Jacob savors the tranquil moment. "I feel the same way. I always love coming out here. Can you believe we are only 30 miles from where we live, but it feels like another world? I could totally see myself living somewhere like this when I'm older. It seems like a great place to write."

"Do you write?" Christine is intrigued.

"Wow, I must feel comfortable with you. I haven't brought that up to anyone else. I keep a journal of the things going on in my life. I'm not sure why I started to do it, but I enjoy writing down my thoughts. It makes me feel better," Jacob confesses.

Christine gently bites her lip. "Well, I hope one day I make it into that journal."

Jacob looks at Christine. "You already have."

"Hopefully this time your uncle doesn't disturb us." Christine's eyes glow as she leans in for a long kiss.

There are certain moments in my life that I wish I could relive. This was definitely one of those sweet times. I can remember the bond that was starting to develop between us. Everything about this relationship felt right. Have you ever met someone and instantly there was an emotional connection? I mean deep-rooted, like your souls had crossed paths prior to knowing each other? That's how I was feeling, and I was hopeful she felt the same way. I had found a friend and partner in crime, someone I could count on. I don't think we were even "officially" dating at that point, but I knew in my heart she would be by my side when I needed her the most. I had told her all about my relationship with my uncle, including things I had never told anyone else. She understood that this barbaric-looking man was one of the most important people in my life. I knew most of my family thought I was crazy for spending time with him; I also knew that to ignore the good in someone because others don't see it was something I would eventually regret. My uncle had emotional issues, but don't we all at some point in our lives? I wasn't yearning for reciprocation of any kind. I was happy to just love him.

"Let's head over to the house before some random weirdo drops off my uncle and we get stuck having to talk to that stranger. The last friend of his I met looked like a 1970s porn star," Jacob warns. He reaches for Christine's hand and leads her to the end of the path.

Christine is awestruck. "Damn, your uncle has his own bridge?"

"He's a high roller, for sure." They giggle. "Believe it or not, there are actually two different bridges that lead to his house. Let's just say we are better off taking this one." Jacob points ahead of them. Christine looks up and salutes with a smirk. "I'll follow your lead, Captain." Holding hands, they stroll across the bridge as the serene atmosphere puts them at ease. Massive oak trees soar high into the air, forming an enchanting, woven covering above the bridge.

After several minutes of lighthearted chit chat, they approach Ostaf's house. They walk up the gravel driveway and stop in front of the porch steps. The dilapidated structure stands as the backdrop of open land surrounds it.

"So, this is the house. Like I said, it's in pretty rough shape. I don't think any work has been done on this place since my uncle moved in. I feel bad for him; it's literally falling apart," Jacob sighs.

Christine looks up at the blue tarp draped over the roof. She notices one of the second story window shutters is dangling by a nail. Concerned, she wonders out loud, "Can someone help him? Is this house even safe to live in?"

"The crazy thing is, he doesn't want help. I don't think he even cares that this place looks the way it does. It's like he's kinda given up on life." Jacob struggles to conceal his tears.

The vicious barking of a nearby dog rumbles through the woods. Panicked, Jacob and Christine turn around and clench each other's arms.

Ostaf shouts out laughing, "It's just me, guys. Calm down! I hope you didn't wet your pants! I'll tell you Jake, you fall for that one every time."

"He's really an 8-year-old boy trapped inside a 44-year-old man's body," Jacob mumbles to Christine.

Ostaf's stomach begins to grumble. "I'm ready for breakfast. I'm *starvin' like Marvin* over here. Did you get me an everything bagel? Those are my favorite.

"You know something, I think there may be one in the bag." Christine is taken aback by the ill-mannered request.

Ostaf's ears perk up like a German Shepherd. "Hold the train! There's only *one*? That's not enough to fill up one of my fingers. Where did you find this girl, Dude?"

Inserting himself into the conversation, Jacob is prompt to intervene: "Relax, Uncle O, it was nice enough that she brought anything. Jeez, where are your manners?"

"Yeah, you sound like my mother. By the way, the house is a little messy. I didn't get a chance to tidy up yet. I just want to let you know before you go inside," Ostaf warns.

"It's fine. Christine will take it easy on you when she does her home inspection. Actually, she left her clipboard in the car, so you got lucky." Jacob's impressed with his own impromptu humor.

After creeping up the unstable steps, everyone enters the house. The putrid smell of rotted food caked onto dirty dishes hovers in the air. Jacob races into the kitchen and turns on the small battery-operated fan in a desperate attempt to camouflage the stench. He flings open several windows to help increase the air circulation.

Ostaf asks, in mid-cough, "Are you hot?"

"Yeah, something like that." Jacob swings open the cabinet doors underneath the sink and rummages through the decade-old stash of cleaning products. He spots a bottle of air freshener and begins to spray like it's a fire extinguisher.

In an effort to distract Jacob's uncle, Christine speaks up: "Who's ready for breakfast?"

Ostaf's Kool-Aid smile is child-like. "Well, it's about time. I don't have all day. Have a seat and let's chow down."

"You know, Uncle O, the weather is beautiful outside. Do you still have that patio set Grandma gave you? We could sit out on your deck and eat." Jacob's face is beet red from the smothering humidity.

Ostaf confirms, "Yeah, I still got it. That's cool. We can sit outside. Do you need me to grab some plates and silverware from the sink?"

"I brought paper plates and plastic forks from the restaurant. We're all good, Uncle O." Christine darts outside through the opened sliding-glass doors.

Ostaf places a cigarette behind his ear. "I'll be there in a few minutes. I got something I want to show you guys."

"OK, but hurry up or I may eat your everything bagel." Jacob shouts as he walks outside onto the creaky deck. The wooden 2x4s are dry-rotted and faded from decades of neglect. He maneuvers around the protruding nails and makes his way to the PVC patio chairs. Sitting down, he lowers his voice, and apologizes to Christine. "I'm so sorry this place smells like hot garbage mixed with morning breath."

Christine giggles. "It's OK. I'm with you. Listen, we all have an Uncle O in our family. Trust me, you're not the only one."

"What sucks is that other than my grandmother, no one else in my family can stand him. And to be honest, I don't think she even has much to do with him nowadays. The entire situation sucks." Jacob peers into the bag of food.

"I got it. I'll make it for you. What do you want?" Christine begins to set up the buffet.

Jacob relaxes. "Wow, that's nice of you. I'll have a plain bagel with some egg salad. Are you sure you don't mind?"

"Of course not. It makes me happy. Why, is that a *crime* or something?" Christine slides the plate with the finished product over to Jacob.

The simple gesture moves him. "Well, thank you very much. That was sweet. I guess I've just never dated anyone like you before."

Christine pulls a scrunchie from her pocket and gathers her hair into a pony tail. "Oh...so, we're dating?" Her playfulness sends Jacob into a tail spin. He struggles to articulate a response. "Um, I mean...yeah... we're dating...I guess...as long as that's OK with you?"

The awkward silence feels like an eternity to Jacob. Christine gets up, walks around the table, and stands in front of him. She looks down, puts her hands on his shoulders and smirks. "Well, Mr. Roth, you know, I don't take that question lightly." With his heart pounding through his chest, Jacob struggles to maintain eye contact. Leaning in further, she whispers into his ear, "Here's the deal...I'll say yes...as long as I know that I'm the *only one* who will be making you a bagel with egg salad."

Jacob holds her hands and plays it cool. "That's a deal." He continues to gaze into Christine's eyes. Just as he moves in for a celebratory kiss, the patio door flies open. Ostaf shuffles onto the deck and lets out a long morning belch. He has several loose cans of beer cradled in his arms and places each one on the table. Ostaf then walks to the edge of the deck and stares into the open field behind his house. He glances at Jacob and smiles.

My uncle didn't think I saw him, but I did. His smile spoke a thousand words. It said, "Even though I'm struggling in my life, I'm grateful that you aren't struggling in yours." It said, "Even though happiness has eluded me, I'm thankful it hasn't missed you." He was more self-aware than anyone gave him credit for. The pain and turmoil that he harbored was buried deep in his core. That day, he was staring far beyond the nature that surrounded his house: he was reflecting on his life. It was a rare moment to see and I'm grateful that I got to witness it.

Ostaf goes into the house again and returns outside holding a larger-size cardboard box that he drops on top of the table. Jacob places his hands on his head. "Oh, shit. That box reminds me, I brought you some great things to sell, Uncle O. I'm sorry. I left them in my car."

Ostaf shakes his head in frustration. "Jake, I've told you so many times. You gotta stop with this. I don't want your stuff. I've got million-dollar inventions sitting in that basement. Ideas that are gonna make a difference in the world one day. Oh, by the way, I've been pulling out some great parts from all those old appliances that people drop off to me. I'll be right back. I wanna show you something really cool I made." Ostaf dashes back into the house to retrieve the top-secret creation.

Jacob updates Christine. "I need to find out more about this actress my uncle claims he dated. I gotta somehow get her first and last name from him. You won't believe this. Remember before when I was digging through his cleaning supplies underneath the sink?"

"Kind of. You were flying around the house. I didn't really see what you were doing." Christine butters her bagel.

Jacob whispers an update. "Well, I saw a plastic bag with a bunch of stuff inside. It looked like there was an address book in there. Actually, I'm shocked he even owns one. I need to snag that before we leave today. Hopefully her number is inside."

Back on the deck, Ostaf plops onto a chair. He has a lit cigarette dangling from his mouth. From inside his shirt pocket, he pulls out a small wooden roller approximately one inch wide with a three-inch-long wooden cylinder handle. He announces, "Check this out...say hello to the *Bagel Roller*! You're probably wondering what this little paint-roller-looking thing does. I need a bagel to show you how this bad boy works." He snatches the everything bagel and slices it horizontally with a knife.

Ostaf beams with pride as he explains the demonstration. "So, this works the best on soft bagels that are fresh out of the oven, but you take this little roller and just start rollin'. Push all that dough down. It's that simple. Roll it around the entire inside of the bagel. When you're done, you have a perfect one-inch-wide groove that is ready to be filled up with something delicious! Personally, I like to go with the egg salad. So...it's officially time to say goodbye to anything ever falling off of your bagel again."

"Wow. That's actually a cool idea, Uncle O. I felt like I was watching one of those infomercials. Do I get a second Bagel Roller free of charge if I order within the next 30 minutes?" Jacob chuckles at his own joke. "Ya know, Uncle O... sometimes the simplest ideas are the home runs. By the way, I'm sorry to tell you, but I ate all the egg salad. It was delish."

"Dude, you better be freakin' joking or you'll get the atomic wedgy again. Chrissy, one day when you're bored, ask your boyfriend about the time I hung him by his underpants outside on a tree branch."

"First of all, her name is Christine, and second, I was like 10 years old. I don't think you would want to try that now, big guy." Jacob jumps up and pokes his uncle's obese belly. The two begin a playful wrestling match and tussle like old times.

Just before Jacob applies his signature finishing move, the full nelson, Ostaf begins gasping for air. He stumbles over to his chair and sits down. Breathing heavy, he places his hand on his chest and leans back. "Fine, I admit it…I can't throw your ass around like I used to."

Jacob is concerned and dashes to his side. "Are you OK, Uncle O? Your face looks pale and you're sweating like you just ran a marathon. What the heck is going on?"

"I'm OK, I'm OK. Just a tad bit out of shape, that's all. I feel perfectly fine. Where the hell is my cigarette? You knocked it out of my mouth, butthead." Ostaf begins to wheeze as he scans the ground looking for his stub.

In an effort to distract his uncle, Jacob changes the subject. "So, what's in the carton you brought out earlier?

Uncle O reaches into the box and pulls out what appears to be a thin, reused, notebook-sized photo album. There is an envelope taped onto the front. He hands it to his nephew and smiles. Jacob opens it and slides the note out. He reads it to himself.

What up Dude?

I can't beleive your eightteen years old.
It seems like just yesterday that
I looked threw the glass window in
the hospitel and saw you for the very
first time, I was so proud to be
your uncle and still I am today. I
know sum times I'm not the easyest
person to deal with. You never
let that change our freindship, thanks
four always being their for me.

I luv you for it! Happy birthday.

Uncle O

Jacob teases Ostaf. "You actually wrote this? Come on. There's no way." He wipes away tears welling in his eyes.

"Huh? Yes…I can actually write. Many don't know that I was a published poet when I was in college." Ostaf clears his throat. "I also did a little writing for the local newspaper when I lived in Idaho, the *Montpelier Tribune*. Some said that my style was similar to Hemmingway."

Jacob hands the card to Christine, then opens the ragged photo album and begins to inspect each page. The pictures are placed in chronological order, from the time Jacob was a newborn through the current year. In one photo, Ostaf is kneeling behind the hospital bassinet with visible pride.

The turn of each album page stirs new emotions that begin to flow through Jacob's body. He is catapulted back in time to a mental montage of special moments with his uncle. From toddler birthday parties, to fishing outings…special childhood memories rush through his mind. Without warning, a specific photo triggers immense emotion. Seven-year-old Jacob is sitting high atop his Uncle O's shoulders. His father, Howard, is standing next to them with his arm around his younger brother. With tears in his eyes, Jacob pushes through and turns each page of the emotional roller coaster. Underneath the last photo in the album, there are three words written by hand with a black marker, TO BE CONTINUED…

"Damn, it's break time for me. This is really intense," Jacob announces as the tears steadily trickle down his face. Christine comforts Jacob by caressing his back. He places his head into his folded arms on the table.

To this day, other than my children being born, that photo album is probably the most special gift I have ever received. In life, we often gauge the quality of a gift by the amount of monetary value it holds. But the priceless ones are the result of the individual giving them having invested their time to create. I probably knew my uncle better than anyone. I also knew that for him to take the time to craft something that beautiful meant he loved me just as much as I loved him. That day the old expression "actions speak louder than words" could not have been truer.

"Happy Birthday, Nephew. I didn't think seeing pictures of my ugly mug would have been such an emotional experience," Ostaf jokes as he cracks open a beer and then starts gnawing away on his bagel.

Jacob lifts his head off the table. "Thanks. This is really special. I'll keep this forever."

"Unfortunately, I couldn't get you a brand-new car like your dad did. I would have liked to have given you something nicer than a photo album," Uncle O confesses mid-cough.

"You know something…sometimes it's things like this that are the best gifts anyone could get." Jacob pats the photo album.

While chewing with his mouth open, Ostaf responds, "I love you, buddy. Like you were my own son. Never forget that. I don't say that about many people. Actually, I can't stand most people. You're a special kid. You always have been." He grabs the crumbs off the table and eats them. "I promise that one day I'll be able to give you something even more special than that album."

Jacob stands up, walks over to his uncle, and attempts to hug him. Startled, Ostaf spins around and makes the accusation. "Hey, are you trying to steal my bagel. I know what you're up to."

Concerned, Jacob looks Ostaf square in the eyes. "Are you sure you're OK? You're sweating through your T-shirt and it's not even that hot outside. It looks like your hands are shaky."

"Dude, I'm fine. Stop. You sound like my mother. I just need to eat something. Sometimes my blood sugar drops if I wait too long. I couldn't feel better. Not to mention, it's a beautiful day and I get to hang with you guys." Ostaf munches on his bagel.

Jacob sits back down. "I'd say let's go inside the house, but it's probably hotter in there than outside."

"I have a bunch of compressors I'm selling this month. Once I get that money, I'm going to get caught up on all of my bills. Trust me, it sucks not having air conditioning in the sweltering summer. Also, the way the sun sets, it hits directly onto my roof. This place feels like a sauna," Ostaf explains as he spots his cigarette on the deck. He picks it up and relights it.

Jacob pulls out an envelope from his pocket. He places it onto the table and pushes it toward his uncle. Caught off guard, Ostaf puts his bagel down. "What's this?" He takes another swig of his beer and belches. Ostaf is speechless as he pulls out 15 crisp $100.00 bills. Astonished, he begins to count each one as the cigarette drops from his mouth again.

"You don't have to wait until next month to pay your bills." Jacob stares into his uncle's tired eyes and smiles.

Ostaf is overcome with emotion. "I can't take this." He places the bills back inside the envelope.

"It was the money I got when my dad sold my old car. I want you to have it," Jacob insists.

Tears pool in Christine's eyes, as well. "You guys…stop it. I can't handle this level of affection. I don't think I can ever come over here again." She grabs a paper napkin and begins to blot around her eyes.

"You caught us on an off day. Normally we can't stand each other," Jacob teases as he walks over and grasps his uncle's shoulders.

Sliding the envelope back, Ostaf reiterates, "Dude, there is *no* way I'm taking this. I'm serious. It's not going to happen."

Jacob doesn't budge. "First of all, you are taking it. That's a direct order, Private. Second, there was a girl holding your hand in one of those pictures you put into the photo album. Who was that?"

"That was Sweet Cheeks. We dated for a few years. She was *a lot* of fun," Ostaf reminisces as he coughs and spits over the deck railing.

Jacob grins. "I'm not even going to ask why you called her Sweet Cheeks. What was her real name? Like what was on her birth certificate?"

"If you want to be technical, it was Janice. She was the gorgeous actress I told you about. I totally forgot that I must have brought her to one of your birthday parties."

Jacob winks at Christine and grins.

"Listen, we gotta get going in a few minutes. Before we hit the road, I'm going to use the bathroom." Jacob holds his stomach.

Ostaf announces the house rule. "Just don't drop a deuce and forget to spray."

"I'll make sure I do it in *your* bathroom and keep the door closed after I'm done," Jacob warns. "Oh…and please don't say anything *creepy* or *disgusting* while I'm gone."

Once inside the house, Jacob goes straight to the kitchen sink and opens the cabinets underneath. He shuffles around the cleaning supplies and finds the white plastic bag. Excited, he looks inside and sees the dust-covered address book.

"Hey! Are you fixing a leak under there?" Ostaf startles Jacob when he opens the freezer door and grabs an Otter Pop. Jacob bumps his head as he attempts to jump up, holding the bag behind his back.

"Um…I was just putting the air freshener back. I did quite a number in your bathroom. The egg salad didn't really agree with me." Jacob puts the plastic bag inside the back of his waist band. Through the kitchen window, he signals Christine to come inside the house while Ostaf's back is turned.

"Listen, we're gonna get rolling, Uncle O. It's getting late." Christine walks inside the house holding the photo album.

Ostaf flails his arms in the air. "Aww, come on, man. There's a ton of cool stuff in my basement I wanna show you. You promised me last time you'd check it out. I have at least five new prototypes you don't even know about."

"Ugh, I know. I'm sorry. We really gotta get going. Listen, next time I see you, we will spend all day down there…I promise. You can show me everything." Jacob feels guilty for cutting the visit short.

Ostaf sulks. "Yeah, sure…next time it is."

"Listen, thanks again for the photo album. I absolutely love it. I'm going to keep it forever and show my kids one day," Jacob imagines as he hugs Ostaf.

"It was so good to meet you, Uncle O. Thanks for having me over, and I hope to see you again soon." Christine follows suit with an affectionate embrace.

Ostaf bellows, "Next time you guys come over I'll have the air conditioning pumping, the house cleaned, and dinner on the table!"

"Sounds like a plan. Just let us know when to be here." Jacob waves goodbye to his uncle and hurries outside with Christine. On the stroll back to the car, Jacob stops and reaches for Christine's hand. He looks her in the eyes and utters the words, "Thank you."

"You don't have to thank me. I should be thanking *you*." She kisses his cheek.

Jacob steps back and tilts his head. "Why would you thank me? You were kind enough to sit through that circus for the last hour."

"I'm only 18 years old and I have a lot of life left to live, but I've *never* seen someone care so much about another person. It's like you see through all of his flaws and try and focus on the good. Most people would *never* give someone like him a chance. You taught me an important lesson today. So, that's why I say…thank you."

Every single time I would visit my uncle it was an adventure. I never knew which way things would go. I guess that was why I enjoyed spending time with him. I was so happy he took that money I gave him. I knew he desperately needed it. It was my way of making sure that he got a small token of what he deserved. I still had not gotten the confirmation I was looking for, but my gut continued to tell me that he got screwed over by my father. The next task I had was to call Sweet Cheeks. But first I had to sit back and bask in the glory of being able to say Christine and I were now officially dating.

Chapter Six

The Search for Sweet Cheeks

• Later that evening •

Pacing, Jacob holds his cordless phone as he waits for Mitch to answer his call.

"Hello, Mitch is busy. He is on the other line with Cindy Crawford. Can I please take your name and number, and his assistant will call you back." the voice answers.

Jacob laughs. "Nice one, man. For a minute you fooled me."

"Did I really?" Mitch asks.

"Um, that would be a no. Listen bro, I got some top-secret intel for you. I mean this is *huge* news. No one knows this. Are you ready?" Jacob's heart rate rises and his mouth becomes dry.

Mitch mocks his friend. "Let me guess, your uncle got pissed again when you wouldn't go into the basement so he could show you his latest award-winning invention?"

"Dude, come on. How is that top-secret intel? OK, I am just going to tell you. It's *official*: Christine and I are dating!" Jacob leaps onto his bed like it's a trampoline and then springs off.

Mitch is flabbergasted. "Holy shit, man! Mazel tov. You weren't kidding, that's big fuckin' news. Listen, I wanna hear more but I gotta go. My mom's boyfriend is on his way over for dinner tonight. I told her I'd eat with them. To be honest, I've never seen her so happy. I hope this guy sticks around. Anyway, I'll call you tomorrow. Let's catch up then."

Jacob hangs up the phone just before there is pounding on his bedroom door and Howard barges in unannounced. "I have some phenomenal news to tell you about, pal! Actually, first let me ask you this: What television station is channel 62?"

Jacob is baffled by the random question. "Um, I'm not sure. Let me check the back of the remote control. I think there's a sticker with all of the channels listed." Pointing on the decal, Jacob confirms, "It looks like channel 62 is Home Shopping Network. Are you buying Mom one of those *Travel Companions*?" Jacob imitates the host of the show. "It's a radio, calculator, and alarm clock all in one. Get yours before they're sold out!" He presses his index finger against his ear like a news reporter and stays in character. "Wait, what's that, Susie? I'm so sorry everyone, we were *just* notified that the *Travel Companion* in the color black is *completely* sold out! WOW! More bad news, loyal at-home shoppers, we only have 40 of the brushed-gray color left in stock. That's it! Grab yours *now* before they're gone!"

"Bravo! That was awesome, Jakey. You're a natural salesman, I tell ya. That gift you got from me. You can thank me another time. Anyway, perhaps I should have you join me when I'm *live* selling my Cool-It on Home Shopping Network's Saturday show, 'Gadget Gifts' with Mary Stevenson!" Howard shouts as he bear hugs Jacob and plants a kiss on his cheek.

Jacob steps back and drops the remote control. "Holy shit, Dad! That's amazing! Congrats! Is it a one-time gig on the show? Oh, and by the way, Mary Stevenson is *really* good looking," Jacob jokes as he maneuvers out of his father's arms.

"Watch it, pal. Now that you're officially dating Christine, you can't be talking like that," Howard teases.

Jacob extends his arm and thrusts his palm onto Howard's chest. "Whoa, wait a minute. How the heck did you know about that? That's private info, Dad."

"I think the next-door neighbors heard you shout it out. Listen, I'm proud of you, bud. I mean that. Things are really coming together for you. College will be starting next month, you have a fantastic girlfriend, and of course that sweet new car. By the way, what did you decide to do with the check I gave you for $1,500?" Howard places his hand on Jacob's shoulder.

"Oh, the check. Yeah, I just deposited it into my savings account. You know me, there's really nothing I need right now," Jacob begins to fidget.

Howard gleams with pride. "Again, I'm proud of you." He exits the room and closes the bedroom door.

Sitting on top of his dresser is the white plastic bag Jacob brought back from his uncle's house. Reaching inside it, he pulls out the yellowed, musty-smelling address book. Jacob mumbles, "Ok, Janice "the famous actress," my uncle better have your number listed in here."

Thumbing through the address book, Jacob flips to the "J" tab. His anxiety skyrockets as he searches through each of the pages. With a fine-tooth comb, he examines every entry as if he is checking for winning lottery numbers. Gritting his teeth, he runs his finger down the last page. The book is slammed closed. "You gotta be kidding me!" Jacob closes his eyes and massages his forehead. Crushed with disappointment, he tosses the book back into the bag, walks into the kitchen, and drops it into the trash can. He trudges back into his room and plops down on his bed. Beat from the action-packed day, Jacob struggles to keep his eyelids open. His head sinks into the feather-filled pillow. His thoughts begin to settle as each breath becomes heavy. Seconds later, his jaw drops open and his head falls to the side.

The telephone ring sounds like a siren and startles Jacob. His eyes flash wide open. Sunlight bursts through the window and covers his face. His digital clock displays 10 a.m. He glances down, clenches his shirt, and kicks off his sneakers. "Holy shit!" Fumbling, he reaches for the phone and answers with a deep, drawn-out yawn, "Hellooo?"

"Good morning, sleepyhead. I guess you're getting all caught up on your beauty sleep," Christine giggles.

Jacob rubs his eyes and chuckles. "Beauty sleep ain't going to help my mug."

"Oh, stop. You and Luke Perry totally could be twins. So, did you ever find your uncle's ex-girlfriend's phone number?" Christine's question is out of genuine interest.

Unable to hide his disappointment and believing he failed, Jacob responds, "Nope…I checked every name in the "J" section. I'm not sure what I'm going to do. She is one of the only people who knows the truth."

"Why were you looking under J? Wasn't she Sweet Cheeks to your uncle?" Christine figured that was so obvious it didn't need to be mentioned.

Like a light switch, Jacob flings himself up. "Holy shit! You're right. Why didn't I think of that? He probably wrote her name and number down under S. Can I call you back? I need to get the phone book out of the trash can."

"Of course. Let me know if you find her number. Talk to you later." Christine hangs up the phone.

Darting out of his room like Carl Lewis, Jacob sprints into the kitchen. He opens the trash can, ready to pull out the address book he had thrown away the night before. Shocked, he sees an empty trash can liner inside.

"Good morning, sweetie. Someone was a tired bear. I hardly saw you at all yesterday. What did you do all day?" Linda inquires with curiosity as she wanders by.

Breathing heavy, Jacob questions, "Mom, what happened to the trash bag that was in here last night? There was something I accidentally threw away that I need."

"Your father just put all the trash into the containers outside. Why? What's with the concerned face? How important could it be?" Jacob's mother asks with a snicker.

Jacob looks up and grits his teeth. "It's important."

Rushing out of the kitchen, Jacob storms outside. He shuffles around the parked cars on the driveway and makes a beeline for the three overfilled trash containers. They are lined up at the curb in preparation for trash pick-up day.

With his hands on his hips, Jacob stares at all the pails. *You gotta be fuckin' kidding me. I'll be here all day.*

Howard pulls into the driveway and honks his horn. He rolls down the car window. "What the heck are you doing, Jakester?" Having already rummaged through several trash bags, Jacob turns around and tries to look natural. He crosses his legs and puts his hands behind his back. "Oh, this? Nothing."

Howard shakes his head as he walks to the house. "Well, you're looking for something. You better clean up this mess before you come back in. Got it?"

"Yeah, OK, Dad." Jacob is ecstatic as he spots the treasure seconds later. Wiping it off with the bottom of his T-shirt, he slides the address book into the waist band of his pants.

Back inside the house, Jacob maneuvers past his parents without being seen and slithers into his room. He closes the door, sits down on his bed and stares at the tattered address book. "Sweet Cheeks, I dug through three-day-old Chinese food for your phone number. *Please* be in here," Jacob grumbles as he looks at his greasy hands.

Sweating bullets, he flips to the S section. He's meticulous, inspecting each name. Adrenaline pumps through his body as he turns each damp page. Suddenly, Jacob spots the blurry name. Bouncing off his bed, he fists pumps the air and grabs his cordless telephone. "Yes! Game time." Rubbing the back of his neck with one hand, he dials the number with the other.

"Hello?" a raspy female voice answers.

Jacob hesitates and then pushes himself to respond. "Hello."

"This better not be a bill collector. I paid my damn car payment this month," the agitated woman lashes out.

Her rough, aggressive personality prompts Jacob to cut her off. "Oh, I'm not looking for your car payment. May I ask if you know someone by the name of Ostaf?"

"Who is this? And tell me why you're calling me," the woman demands.

Sounding apologetic, he answers, "My name is Jacob Roth. I'm Ostaf's nephew."

Janice's demeanor instantly changes. "Oh…how are you, honey? Of course, I know your uncle and I even remember you, too."

Jacob exhales. "I'm so sorry for bothering you. I really am."

"My God, did Ostaf love you, Jacob. You were his entire world when I knew him. The joy in his eyes every time you ran over to him was like nothing I had ever seen. You know your uncle wasn't the type to show emotion, but boy, oh boy, when it came to you, that wasn't the case. How is he doing, sweetheart?" Janice is eager for an update.

There's silence as Jacob thinks back to his recent visits. "He is hanging in there. I'm a little worried about his health. He doesn't take care of himself like I wish he would. I feel like part of him has just given up on life. It's sad." Jacob's voice flutters as he expresses his sorrow.

"I know what you mean. I was always worried about him. The drinking and the smoking were non-stop. That was one of the reasons we ended up going our separate ways." She sighs. "So, tell me, has he invented his million-dollar product yet?"

Jacob is elated. "It's funny you asked me that. It's actually the reason that I'm calling you. Do you happen to have a few minutes to talk to me? I mean…I can call you back if now isn't a good time."

"Honey, I'm all ears. I got nowhere to go. I'm very happy to talk to you and answer any questions you have." Her kindness puts Jacob at ease.

He sits down and leans back against his dresser. "Well, thank you very much. I'll try to keep this simple and to the point. My uncle still hasn't invented anything worth anything. So that hasn't changed. However, my father has recently invented a product that he patented. It sounds like this one could be the million-dollar invention in the family. He's already signed a huge purchase agreement with Walmart and is going on Home Shopping Network with it. I have a feeling it is going to make my father *a lot* of money."

"That's fantastic, sweetie. I liked Howard. Even though your uncle and father never got along, I always knew that Ostaf wanted your father to be proud of him. But that's a story for another day. So, tell me, what is the product?" Janice's interest is genuine.

Jacob describes the invention. "It's a plastic sports drink bottle that has a removable blue ice cartridge that hangs down from the top. So, you basically freeze that piece and it keeps your drink cold without any ice. No more watered-down drinks."

"Wow. That sounds like a really great product. Please tell your dad I said congratulations," Janice responds.

"I sure will." He braces himself for the finale. "You know my uncle exaggerates the truth sometimes, right?" Jacob asks, trying to not sound judgmental.

Janice laughs. "Sometimes? You're being very kind, sweetie. It was most of the time. Let's be honest. He would tell everyone I was a famous actress for years. The truth was, back in high school I did a few television commercials. Local ones at that…if they even aired. But yes, he would 'bend' the truth."

"Well, my uncle told me that in 1987 he met my father at a deli. Which I have to say…that alone is wild, considering they can't stand being around each other. Anyway…he said that he showed up with a sketch of something he had created." Jacob paces while he explains the story's timeline.

Janice giggles and adds, "Oh yes, the *sketches.* I think he had hundreds of them. All stored neatly in binders. Actually, that was the only organized thing in his life. There's gotta be a hidden gem in there somewhere. You know, like a needle in a haystack, as they say. If they even still exist."

"Well, the sketch he brought to show my father that day may have been the one. My uncle told me that *he* created the entire design and my father promised him money if it ever sold." Jacob's emotion builds as he reveals the sensitive details.

Janice asks, "Did that ever happen?"

"No, not one red cent. My father hasn't said a word to my uncle about anything going on right now with his product. I mean *literally* nothing. The reason I called you was to see if you knew the truth. You were his girlfriend back then. Do you know if what my uncle said was true? I need any details I can get before I confront my father. I can't stand by and see my uncle get taken advantage of anymore." A sense of despair is evident in Jacob's voice. "Hello, are you still there?" The seconds of silence feel like minutes.

"I'm still here, honey." Janice's tender tone defuses the conversation. "You're a good person. I'm sure you've been told that many times. You seem to have a lot of compassion for your uncle. But, I'm sorry, Jacob. I don't remember if that really happened. I have no memory of him ever telling me about that idea."

Jacob's head hangs low and he taps his fist against the top of the dresser. "That's OK. It was worth a try. I'll just have to follow what's in my heart. Hopefully that will lead me to the truth."

"I think that is a beautiful way to look at this situation, Sweetie. Listen, you take care of yourself. I'm glad you called me. It was so good to hear your voice."

Looking into the mirror, Jacob's dejected eyes stare back. "It was good to hear yours, too. Take care. Bye." The phone drops from his hand and he rips apart the address book. With a heavy grunt, he falls back onto his bed and curses at the ceiling.

As the old saying goes, the truth hurts. It was time I started to accept that this was just another episode of *Storytelling with Ostaf*. People are who they are; my father was right in that regard. I know my uncle didn't have any malicious intent when he would share his tall tales. I truly believe that part of him just wanted his fantasies to become his realities. He was always looked at as "the brother who never accomplished anything" and he was tired of it. However, I was able to see the complete opposite. Sometimes the biggest success we can achieve is making a positive impact on someone else's life. My uncle had done that for me. It was time I just embraced that and put this investigation to bed.

Chapter Seven

Health Scare

• Two weeks later •

T he television blares in the background. Jacob pulls out the cherished photo album Ostaf had given him. He is sitting on the floor, fascinated by the pictures his uncle placed inside the pages. He focuses on every detail, every memorialized moment in time. Memories are triggered and Jacob closes his eyes. There is a bang on the door.

"Yeah?" Jacob slams the photo album closed.

Howard peers into the room and mumbles as he chews a piece of corned beef. "What's going on? What are you up to?"

"Not much. I'm just watching the movie *Somewhere in Time.* It's on HBO again. Jacob slides the photo album underneath his bed.

Howard is beaming. "That's a great movie. One of my favorites. I love the soundtrack." He shares a big announcement. "I wanted to tell you I signed the NCAA licensing agreement today. It's official! We have the rights to put 30 of the top college logos on the container. This is big news, pal."

"Sweet, Dad. That's amazing. Nice job. You always work hard to accomplish your goals." Jacob mutes the TV.

Howard fist pumps. "It's all about being passionate and loving what you do. If you're not passionate about it, don't do it. You'll never win if you take on something you don't love. It's how I try and live my life, Jacob. Remember, at the end of the day, it's what you accomplish that matters. I always say there's a difference between a *day dreamer* and a *dream chaser*. You're the latter. That's why you're going to kick some butt in college and make a lot of money one day.

Jacob asks with sincerity, "Dad, do you think making a lot of money is what life is about? Does it really matter how big your savings account is if you're not happy?"

"Listen, pal. Money isn't the only path to happiness, but not having it brings its own stress. Trust me on that one. Look at your uncle. I just want you to win at whatever you decide to do." Howard clears his throat. "Speaking of money, last month's bank statement came in the mail. I noticed you never deposited the check I gave you for your birthday. I thought you were putting that into your savings account. Where is it?" Howard rubs his chin.

Jacob responds, "Oh, that...I just haven't gotten around to depositing it yet. I've been busy. It's on my to-do list."

"I just hope you haven't given any of that money to your uncle. That was for you...only." Howard turns his head away.

Jacob is perturbed by the accusation. "Dad...and what if I did? What would be so bad if I helped someone in need?"

"I've told you a hundred times. You can't help someone who doesn't want to help themselves, bud. Unfortunately, your uncle has caused everyone in this family nothing but stress and aggravation for many years. We've all tried to help him. After a while you just lose your patience." Howard walks out of Jacob's bedroom.

The phone rings. Irritation with his dad is evident in his voice when Jacob answers, "Hello?"

"What's going on? Are you OK? You sound pissed off." Christine sits down and gets comfortable, preparing to listen with focus.

Jacob takes a deep breath. "I just have a lot running through my mind right now. College starts in three weeks, my dad just pissed me off, and I'm really worried about my uncle's health."

"I'm sorry. You have a lot that you're dealing with. I want to hear what's going on with your uncle, but do you want to call me back?"

Jacob uses his finger to draw a heart shape in the carpet. "It's OK. I always want to talk to you. Just hearing your voice puts me in a better mood."

"Awww, that is so sweet." Christine places her hand on her chest. "I feel the same way about you, too. Tell me, how is your uncle?"

"I haven't told anyone yet. My grandma called me earlier. He had to go to the hospital today because he was having chest pains. They also found at least two ulcers on his intestines. He's a mess."

"Oh my God. I'm so sorry. How is he feeling? Where is he now?" Christine rattles off questions with concern.

"Thankfully he seems to be doing all right. He's back at his house. My grandma said he's even been down in his basement working on some new prototype sketches."

Christine exhales. "Well, that's good news. I'm glad to hear he's doing better. What did the doctor say caused the chest pains?"

"They did an EKG. My grandmother said that he has something called "mild heart rhythm abnormalities." Say that diagnosis five times. I had to write it down. Anyway, they want to schedule a nuclear stress test, but his insurance doesn't cover it. Now I'm even more happy I gave him that money. You know, my grandmother hasn't even told my father yet. I was going to give him the news, but he pissed me off with *another* lecture right before you called. I really wonder if he would have even cared."

"I'm sure he would have. At the end of the day Ostaf is still his little brother. Who knows, maybe one day they will work things out. You never know." Christine shrugs. Her optimism is uplifting for Jacob.

Jacob continues, "You may be the first person to ever use the word "little" when speaking about my uncle. You're always so positive. I really love that about you. My uncle thinks I hit the lottery when we started hanging out. He keeps telling me I better not screw things up between us. I don't think I've ever heard him speak so highly about another person before."

"That's really sweet. And he's right: you better not screw things up." Christine is only half-joking. "Listen, I have to go.

My parents want to take me out for dinner tonight since I'll be leaving for school in another couple of weeks."

Deflated, Jacob replies, "Yeah, that's right…school. It's right around the corner.

"We will figure things out. I promise. I gotta go. I'll call you tomorrow." Christine hangs up the phone.

I have to admit, I wasn't surprised at all about my uncle's health. All you had to do was watch the way he lived his life. It was so hard to believe that he was only 44 years old, because he looked 64. I was praying that this health scare would wake him up. Maybe he would start taking better care of himself. He was smoking more than a chimney and drinking non-stop. My grandmother told me that this was the first time he had his blood tested in almost 20 years. Living like a hermit on a secluded island had caught up to him.

It was a stressful time for me, especially knowing that Christine and I would be attending different schools. We were going to be leaving in the next two weeks and we had hardly discussed it. I guess neither one of us wanted to bring it up since things were going so well. The one positive was that we would only be about two hours away. We would see each other on weekends and holidays. It's sad to say, but part of me wondered if we would even stay together through our freshman year. I mean, college is another world and commitments sometimes go out the window once you land on campus. I was really starting to care about her. It seemed like she felt the same way about me. Even though I was the happiest I had ever been, I was still filled with anxiety. Most of that was because I knew my uncle was sinking further into a depression. I had to try to cheer him up and make sure he was OK before I left for school.

• The Next Day •

It's a peaceful Sunday afternoon. The sun's golden rays blast down like lasers from the tranquil blue sky. Floating on a pool raft, Jacob is wearing his Ray-Ban sunglasses and a wide-brim sunhat. His eyes are closed and he is napping as the sound of the pool filter flutters in the background. Startling him awake, there is banging on the patio door that sounds like thunder.

Jacob's eyes flash wide open as he tumbles off the raft and splashes into the water. He shouts, "Jesus Christ, Dude, you scared the shit out of me! I was half asleep."

Mitch laughs as he walks outside and sits down on a chaise lounge. "What's going on, man. I haven't heard from you in days. You doing all right?"

Holding onto the ledge of the pool, Jacob gets his bearings. "Yeah, I'm good." He holds his nose and dunks his head backward into the water. "It's just been a crazy last few weeks. Of course, it's all happening right before I leave for school."

Mitch puts on his sunglasses. "So, what's going on? Fill me in."

"Well, for starters, my uncle had to go to the hospital because he was having chest pain. They also found ulcers on his intestines. The doctor wants to do a nuclear stress test on him. I'm not even sure what the hell that is, but it sounds scary." Jacob doesn't try to hide his concern.

Mitch nods and confirms, "That's definitely the test you want him to have. They'll inject him with a radioactive dye that shows the blood flow of his heart muscle. The technician usually takes two sets of images—one while he's resting and one after exertion. The easiest way to explain it is…if he has any blockages or narrowed arteries, that test will show it."

Jacob is amazed and compliments his friend. "Thanks, man. You're gonna be a great doctor one day. You get so freakin' passionate when you speak about anything having to do with medicine."

"I appreciate that. You know, it's funny, when you love something, it's not really work. If someone will pay me to do something I would do for free, I won the game of life. I mean, isn't that everyone's dream?" Mitch reclines in the lounge chair.

Jacob agrees. "Absolutely. It's funny: my father always says the same thing. I just hope that one day I'll find my passion."

"You already have." Mitch smiles.

Jacob doesn't understand. "I have?"

"Of course, bro. You love helping people. You care about people. One day that will translate into your career in some way. You'll see," Mitch encourages.

Filled with gratitude, Jacob takes a deep breath and exhales. "You're a good friend, man. I'm so glad we will be at the same college this fall. Especially since Christine won't be there."

"It will all work out. Don't worry." Mitch places his hands behind his head. "Oh, I almost forgot to tell you: Dean Chapman bought a car from my father. And…get this: I had a *private tour* of the campus last week. It was incredible. I met a bunch of the professors. Each one was cooler than the last. And wait until you see the rec hall. It was filled with tons of arcade games. They even have Mortal Kombat and NBA Jam. We are gonna *love* going there," Mitch proclaims as he imitates WWE's Ric Flair. "Whoooo!"

"Damn, that's amazing! I can't believe you didn't tell me about the tour. It's kind of a big deal," Jacob teases.

Mitch leaps up and apologizes. "Sorry, man. I've just been so busy getting ready for school. Listen, I gotta run. My dad is taking me to Bed, Bath, and Beyond. I gotta get the rest of the stuff for my dorm room. He's all excited that he found a bunch of those 20-percent-off coupons. Call me later."

"Sounds good. Make sure you have your dad buy the mini fridge and microwave. Oh, and tell him we need a blender for protein shakes," Jacob jokes and winks.

"They're already on the list, my man." Mitch gives a thumbs up and hustles through the open patio door.

Soon after, Jacob gets out of the pool, grabs his towel, and dries off. He walks inside just as the phone begins ringing. Leaving wet footprints on the tile floors, he shuffles into his room and grabs the receiver. On his caller ID, Jacob sees a familiar number displayed. Grinning, he's quick to take the call. He blurts out, "Yo! What's going on? Where the heck are you calling me from?"

"Dude, I'm calling you from my house! Thanks to you I'm caught up on all my bills. The air conditioning is humming, the roof leaks are fixed and the blue tarp is gone…and you won't believe this one: I actually hired a company to come over and clean my house. The place looks *marvelous*!" Ostaf tap dances in jubilation.

Jacob beams with pride. "That's amazing! Really, that makes me happy. I'm so pumped to see the place."

"Well, that's the reason I'm calling you. You know I *always* keep my promises. I'd like to invite you and your lovely lady over for a fine dining experience at El Ostaf's. I was thinking perhaps you could both come over next Saturday evening. There's a great Italian restaurant nearby that delivers. I gave them a freezer compressor in exchange for a food credit. Their chicken cacciatore and rigatoni are delizioso." Ostaf voices an impressive Sicilian accent.

Jacob is honored to receive the invite. "That sounds awesome. I was actually going to ask you about having dinner together. I'm free, but let me check with Christine tomorrow. I am sure she would love to come over. We can make it my going-away-to-school dinner."

"Totally! Dude, you won't recognize the house. Not only does it look great, but it smells clean." Ostaf lights a cigarette. "Um, you do know I was in the hospital this week with chest pains?"

"Of course I know. I was just going to ask how you're feeling. Thankfully you sound good," Jacob says, relieved.

Ostaf responds, "Well, you're right. I am feeling a lot better, thankfully. But guess who never called me?"

"Who?" Jacob prepares himself for the tirade.

Ostaf snaps back. "Your father, that's who!"

"Well, that sucks. I'm sorry to hear it. Maybe he doesn't know you have your phone line working again." Jacob attempts to justify the situation.

"He knows. Our mother told him. Anyway, I'm used to it. After 40 years it just becomes what it is. At least I can always count on you." Ostaf flicks his cigarette in an ashtray.

With no hesitation, Jacob responds, "Right back at ya."

"Listen, I've been sketching out something really cool. It's gonna be completely different than anything else I've ever invented. I'll show you when I see you on Saturday. I love you." Ostaf hangs up the phone.

Jacob mumbles to himself, "I love you, too, Uncle O."

• The Next Day •

The car windows are down and the sunroof is open. The song "Sailing" by Christopher Cross is playing on the radio. The wind is blowing through Jacob's hair as he drives. He pulls into the driveway, puts his car in park, and honks the horn. He gets out and opens the passenger door as Christine frolics out of her house. Jacob greets her with an embrace and a kiss on her forehead.

"It's so crazy: it's only been two days since I saw you and it feels like it's been weeks. Once school starts, it will be weeks that we don't see each other. Those weeks are gonna feel like years. I just know it." Jacob sighs and caresses Christine's face.

She looks up at Jacob, happy to be standing next to him. "Well, let's just make the most of the time we have together before school starts. Can we do that?"

Jacob leans back with Christine in his arms. "Yes, we can. By the way, you won't believe who *officially* invited us over for dinner on Saturday night."

Christine straightens Jacobs collar. "And who would that be?"

"Before I tell you, just know that there will be air conditioning, the place will smell clean, and the food will be brought in." Jacob makes himself laugh.

"I'm going to go out on a limb and say we would be going to your uncle's." Christine struggles to keep a straight face.

High-fiving Christine, Jacob pretends to hold a microphone. "I am excited to announce that you just won the grand prize with that guess."

"Oh, yeah, what prize did I win?" She runs her finger down Jacob's chest.

He gulps and does his best game-show host impression. "You, my lovely lady, get to spend an enchanting evening at El Ostaf's with yours truly. I mean, it doesn't get better than that." They laugh in unison. "It's funny, actually. He's taking this dinner invite *very* serious. When I spoke to him today, he told me that he used the money I gave him to fix the roof leaks, pay all his bills, and hire a cleaning company for the house. I couldn't believe it."

"Awww, that is so cute. Your uncle wants you to be proud of him. He loves you *so* much." Christine stands on her tip-toes and kisses Jacob on the lips.

"I just want him to be healthy and happy. That's all. So, are you good with dinner Saturday night at my uncle's?" Jacob holds up his hands and crosses his fingers.

Christine pouts. "I would have loved to go, but my cousin has her bridal shower that afternoon down in South Jersey. I won't be back in time. I'm so sorry. You know I totally would have gone."

"I know you would have. Don't worry about it. He'll miss seeing you, for sure. Jacob's smile camouflages his disappointment.

Christine shares a back-up plan. "Come over after you leave his house. I should be home by then. I'll grab a movie at Blockbuster for us on my way back. There's a bunch of new releases. I really want to see *Wayne's World* or *Batman Returns*. I hope they have them in stock. When I went on Tuesday, every single copy they had was checked out. It's so annoying. I even stood at the drop-off slot like an idiot, asking people which movie they were bringing back."

"Wow. That's dedication right there. Any chance we can go with a classic like *Back to the Future* or *The Goonies*? Please? I'll bring you Twizzlers." Jacob is fierce with his negotiations.

Playfully poking Jacob's chest, Christine offers a compromise: "Only if you promise not to fall asleep and leave me watching the movie by myself. Like you do *every* time. Do you remember last week when you made me watch *The Karate Kid*? You were out cold before Mr. Miyagi fixed Daniel's bike."

"OK, OK, I won't fall asleep," Jacob promises as he puts his head on Christine's shoulder, closes his eyes, and begins to snore.

I was bummed that Christine couldn't go to my uncle's for dinner, but I was excited to see him. I knew once I started college, all the extra time I had would be gone. I was going to do everything I could to enjoy this last dinner with him before I left. It's funny—I can still remember the pride in his voice when he told me all his bills were paid and his house was clean. It reminded me that one of the most selfish acts in life is to actually help someone else out. It's selfish because of the joy *you* get in return when that person benefits from your kindness. Giving him that money was probably one of the most rewarding things I have ever done. To this day, I'm grateful my 18-year-old self knew what love and compassion was.

Chapter Eight
Bon Voyage Dinner

• Saturday •

With the garden hose in his hand, Jacob is enjoying the early afternoon breeze as he sprays the soapsuds off of his car.

As he comes out the front door, Howard shouts, "She's looking great, pal. There's not a spot of dirt on her. WOW! I tell ya... anything you do is always done with excellence. I'm proud of you, buddy. You get that from me. Hey, for old times' sake...What are the three Roth Rules I taught you back when you were just a little guy?"

"Come on, Dad. I'm trying to just relax out here. I'm not bothering anyone." Jacob rolls his eyes.

Howard doesn't give up. "You know it makes me happy. One last time, for me. Come on."

"Set a goal, work hard, and never quit. There. I said it," Jacob mumbles and sprays his father with the water hose. Howard attempts to take cover behind a tree. Jacob stalks him holding the nozzle. "OK, you got me. I give up!" Howard shouts as he puts his hands up in the air and shuffles backwards.

Jacob teases, "I haven't seen you move that fast in years. Also, why are you wearing khakis, a long-sleeve dress shirt, and loafers when it's 98 degrees outside?"

"Don't worry about what I'm wearing, OK? Live and let live. What are you doing tonight?" Howard probes as he rolls up his sleeves.

111

Jacob hesitates. "Going over to Uncle O's for dinner. Please don't give me shit about it, Dad. I'm serious. I'm not in the mood to get into an argument with you."

"I'm not going to say anything. You're an adult now. If spending time with him makes you happy, then good for you. Oh, I need you to do me a favor. I have something for you to give him today when you're over there. I left it on my desk. It will save me a stamp. Please *do not* open it. Just hand it to him on your way out and don't discuss anything. Got it?"

Jacob wonders what shenanigans his father is up to. "Yeah, I will."

"What time are you leaving?" Howard grabs the towel and dries his face.

Jacob answers as he turns off the hose. "Around five o'clock. I'm going to stop and pick up dessert on the way over."

"That's nice of you. Is Christine going?" Howard continues the cross-examination.

Jacob groans, "What's with the interrogation, Dad? My God. No, she's not going. She's at a bridal shower. Come on, man."

Howard's tone is obnoxious. "Lucky her. Oh, and by the way, I gave you a sample of the Cool-It with the Ohio State logo on it. I put it on top of your dresser. It looks fantastic." He scurries inside the house and closes the door.

• Later that day •

Jacob grabs a bottle of water from the fridge before leaving to go to his uncle's house. "You look handsome, honey," Linda compliments.

"Oh, thanks, Mom. I just threw on some jeans and a shirt. Nothing fancy." Jacob reaches for a Lunchable inside the refrigerator.

His mother comments, "Smart idea. You should definitely make sure you eat something before you go to your uncle's house for dinner. God only knows what he plans to serve you."

"Stop! That's not why I'm having a snack, Mom. I'm just hungry. Jeez. Anyway, he's bringing in food. He's excited for this. It's probably the last time I'll see him for a while," Jacob explains as he chews a mouthful of crackers and cheese.

Linda walks over and places her palms on Jacob's cheeks. "Have a good time."

"Thanks, Mom. I will. I gotta run. I'm supposed to be over around six o'clock." Jacob leaves the house and unlocks his car. Just as he sits down, he realizes he forgot Howard's special delivery. Back in the house, Jacob creeps into his father's office and spots the envelope for Ostaf. The words "For You!" are written on the front. He slides it into his back pocket, walks outside, and gets into his car. After starting the ignition, Jacob inserts his Mr. Mister CD. The song "Broken Wings" plays as he drives away.

For me, there is nothing better than cranking up the music, opening the car windows, and cruising down a highway to one of my favorite songs. Let's also throw in a cool evening breeze and it's absolutely perfect. Do you have that *one* song that immediately takes you to that euphoric place? You know, where it triggers the emotions of the past and present at the same exact time? I had plenty of feelings running through my mind that night.

On one hand, I was happy and excited. Having a beautiful girlfriend and the thrill of starting college was incredible. At the same time, I was being emotionally pulled in another direction.

All I could think about was my uncle. I knew that once I left for college my relationship with him would never be the same. I had the foresight to know that leaving meant new friends, road trips with the guys, and spending time with Christine. I just didn't see my uncle in the picture and it made me really sad. I didn't want it to be like that, but I knew in my heart this dinner was going to be my farewell in its own way.

After stopping at the local bakery, Jacob begins the routine expedition toward Ostaf's house.

As dusk sets in, the sunset's pastel colors wrap around the horizon. When he arrives, Jacob takes a deep breath and grabs the dessert from his back seat. The colossal spruce trees lining the gravel-covered path resemble a landscape painting. In the far-away distance, lights shine through the windows of Ostaf's house.

"Alright: electricity! Well, that's a good thing," Jacob mumbles as he begins the peaceful trek. As he steps onto the path, Jacob notices an abandoned tractor. He climbs onboard and sits down.

I never knew what type of household appliances or farming machinery I would stumble upon when I would visit my uncle. That evening, the 1955 Farmall 200 seemed like a nice place to take a break and unwind for a few minutes. I remember leaning back and kicking my feet up onto the steering wheel. (There's also a good chance I may have tasted the cheesecake to make sure it was up to par.)

From where I was sitting, I could see light coming from the basement windows. I hated imagining what kinds of things were stored down there. For my uncle, time stood still, probably because he almost never left his property. He believed it had only been a few months since I saw his workshop, but it was actually approaching two years. The reason I always put it off was because I just didn't care. Seeing his newest inventions and sketches and having to hear about them was a nuisance. It was like listening to the teacher in the Charlie Brown episodes: painful. I am sure he could see the boredom on my face, but he never stopped smiling each time he had something new to show me.

During the last few months of that summer, I became intrigued each time he would talk to me about a new idea. Maybe it was because I was getting older and could appreciate his passion to create. His imagination began to fascinate me. It was like this river of ideas that never stopped flowing through his mind. Few things brought my uncle joy and I knew hanging out in his laboratory that night would be a special memory we would both always remember.

Approaching the house, Jacob notices the tarp that was covering the roof is no longer there. The patches of grass in the front yard have been freshly cut. Newly purchased wind chimes create angelic percussion as they dangle from the porch ceiling.

Jacob is astounded by the transformation. "Wow. Would you look at this! He's not messing around. This place looks awesome." Jacob notices that each wooden step has been nailed firmly into place.

Upon opening the front door, a delicious aroma gets his attention. The entire house has been organized. All of the run-down furniture and random mechanical parts are no longer there. The wooden floors are swept and the carpet has been cleaned.

Jacob does a double-take. "This place looks amazing, Uncle O! I'm telling you...I would never know it's the same house." In the kitchen, the table is set with folded napkins and silverware. The tins of food sit on the counter, waiting to be opened.

"Everything looks great! I can't wait to dig into this feast. By the way, I picked up your favorite cheesecake from Ronnie's Bakery. It's the one with the graham-cracker crust that you like. I even asked them to put the berries on the side." Jacob smiles in anticipation of Ostaf's response. He places the scrumptious dessert on the table. Through the hallway, Jacob hears the television in his uncle's dimly lit bedroom. Ostaf is lying on the couch.

"Dude, get up. Time for dinner." Jacob flicks on the light switch.

Nudging his uncle, Jacob repeats, "Come on. Get up. Nap time is over. We need to eat dinner, big guy. The food is going to get cold and I'm starving." Jacob turns off the TV. "I'm excited to check out the basement after dinner. I want to see that new sketch you were telling me about."

Bent down on one knee, Jacob stares at Ostaf's face. "I'm telling you, if you're messing with me, you're gonna get it. This isn't funny." He lifts and drops his uncle's arm.

Fear sets in and ravages Jacob's body. His heart rate skyrockets as he examines his uncle's motionless chest. With his trembling hand placed on Ostaf's face, perspiration seeps through Jacob's shirt. Each breath becomes heavier as his emotions begin to spiral. Jacob demands, "Wake up, now! You better be joking around. I'm not kidding…. You're actually scaring me."

While he gently shakes his uncle, tears begin to trickle down Jacob's face. Panic sets in as Ostaf lies lifeless. Jacob begs, "Please wake up, Uncle O. This is our special dinner. It's the last one we will have before I leave for college." Struggling to catch his breath, Jacob places two fingers onto the side of his uncle's neck. Time stands still as he holds Ostaf's hand and waits.

Jacob whispers into his uncle's ear and then unleashes a blaring scream.

Devastating. That's the only word that comes to mind when I think about losing my uncle. That night a piece of me died with him. The intense shock shook my soul. I knew he had been struggling with health issues but never did I think it would have ended up the way it did. The autopsy results showed that the cause of death was something called "hypertrophic cardiomyopathy." It's a genetic disease that causes the heart muscle to grow abnormally thick. No one knew he had it. Over time it restricted his blood flow to his heart. In simple terms, his heart was working two to three times harder than it should have been. Throw in the 30 years of smoking and drinking, and it was a recipe for disaster. The day his heart gave out…mine crumbled into a million pieces. I am still picking them up to this day.

Chapter Nine

From the Other Side

• One week later — Saturday morning •

L ounging on his bed, Jacob is watching *Stand by Me* when his phone rings. He pushes himself to answer.

"Hey, how are you doing?" Christine asks.

Jacob hesitates. Emotionless, he replies, "It's not getting any easier. I don't know how I'll be able to leave for school next week. I really don't." He takes a deep breath. "That night just keeps replaying in my mind. It's like a nightmare that I can't wake up from."

"I feel so bad. I should have been there with you. No one should have to deal with something like that by themselves. Do you feel up to going to the mall with me? You can totally say no." Christine hopes they can spend the day together.

Jacob smiles. "Of course I'll go. The only time I'm in a good mood lately is when I'm with you."

"You're so sweet. What if I pick you up in…let's say an hour? Oh, and if you're a good boy, I'll buy you an Orange Julius when we get there." Christine knows his weaknesses.

Grinning, Jacob bargains, "Can I also get a slice of pizza from Sbarro?"

"I'll buy you two. See you in a little bit," Christine says, looking forward to their day together.

Jacob trudges over to his closet and reaches into his laundry basket. Digging through his dirty clothes, he searches for his favorite pair of jeans. At the bottom of the basket he spots them. Yanking them out, the envelope that he never gave Ostaf drops out of the back pocket.

Stunned, Jacob mutters to himself, "My God, I totally forgot about that."

Contemplating whether he should open the envelope, he recalls his father's order not to. An emotional tug-of-war plays out in Jacob's mind. He looks down and scratches the back of his head. *Damn, what should I do?* he wonders. He stares at the envelope for several minutes. The buildup of anticipation is irresistible. Jacob is careful as he unseals the flap. He pulls out a small piece of paper. Three words are written down. "I owe you." Confused by the cryptic message, Jacob sees another small piece of paper inside the envelope. It's folded in half. Pacing back and forth, he debates unfolding it.

As the internal struggle continues, Jacob mumbles, "Sorry, Dad. I need to know what this is about." Closing his eyes and taking a deep breath, Jacob nervously unfolds the paper. Looking down, he realizes he's holding a business check. It is made out to Ostaf. Glancing at the line below, Jacob sees that it is written in the amount of $37,000.00. Staggering, he shouts, "Holy shit!" as he zooms down and looks at the bottom left corner of the check. The memo line says the payment is for: Product royalties.

Jacob's eyes widen as he stumbles backward. He places his hand on his chest and gathers himself. Tears well in his eyes as the realization of his uncle's truth and his father's integrity overwhelms him. "Well, I guess you wanted me to know, Uncle O." Jacob grabs the Cool-It from his dresser and flips the container into the air. He catches it, and smiles.

> Well, my search for the truth had come to an end. I realized early in my life that when things like this happen, you can't write it off as coincidence. Had those jeans ended up in the washing machine like they should have, I would never have seen that envelope. My uncle wanted me to know the truth. Even more special and selfless, he wanted me to know my father kept his word. Just when I thought things couldn't have gotten any more intense or emotional, they did.

The telephone rings. Jacob takes a deep breath and exhales slowly. He lumbers over and answers. "Hello?"

"Hi, honey. Do you have a few minutes to talk?"

"Of course. How are you doing, Grandma?"

"I'm OK, my dear grandson. How are you doing?...I want you to know your uncle would tell me all the time how special you were to him," Jacob's grandmother reminisces.

With a little sarcasm, Jacob comments, "Hey, he never told *me* that."

"Oh, sweetheart, he did. Through his actions. Your uncle was so proud of that picture album he made you. It took him almost a month to finish it. He went through many boxes of photographs to find *just* the right ones. For your 18th birthday he had always wished he could have given you more."

Jacob whimpers and struggles to respond, "But Grandma, he gave me one of the most special gifts I have ever gotten—that photo album."

"He is going to give you one more gift, Jacob. Several months ago, he updated his will. It was one of the few things he did not procrastinate with. He wanted you to have his house and everything inside of it. All of those inventions, he wanted you to have them. He knew that if there was even *one* that could make the world a better place, you would find it— you would bring it to life when the time was right."

Overcome with emotion, Jacob places the phone on mute as he gathers his composure. "Wow…I don't even know what to say, Grandma. I'm sorry, but I have to go. I'll call you later. I love you."

Jacob throws himself down on his bed and buries his face in his pillow. He attempts to process the immense gift that Ostaf has left him.

I know it sounds odd to say, but I feel like my uncle knew he was going to be leaving this world when he did. I vividly remember walking up to the house the night we were supposed to have our dinner. It looked so beautiful. He had worked so hard. It was almost like he was preparing the house for something…big.

Chapter Ten

Uncovered Brilliance

• The next day — Return to Ostaf's •

J acob pulls into Mitch's driveway and honks the horn. Dashing out of his house, Mitch opens the passenger door, gets in, and fist-bumps Jacob. "What's up, bro? You sure you're up to this?"

"I'm gonna have to go inside again at some point. Might as well do it before I leave for school." Jacob preps himself for the emotional return.

Mitch tries not to sound uncaring. "When does the house "officially" become yours?"

"I'm not sure. My dad is taking care of the legal stuff. I just want to get anything out of there that's important before we rent it. You know something?…I never made it into the basement." The guilt rests uneasy in Jacob's heart.

"I know how badly he wanted to spend time with you down there. I'm sure there's some really cool stuff he was working on." Mitch buckles his seatbelt.

Jacob backs onto the street. "Let's go find out." He turns up the radio, opens the windows, and begins the emotional return.

• At the house •

"Wow. This place looks great," Mitch says. "Amazing what some yard work and landscaping can do. You guys did a nice job cleaning it up for the renters."

Jacob clarifies, "My uncle did all of that. He even secured the porch steps. They're actually safe to walk on now. And the roof…check it out. No blue tarp. All the roof leaks are fixed. One of his wacky flea-market friends is a handyman. I'm guessing he helped my uncle with a lot of this work.

"It's wild that he had all this done right before he passed away. I mean, he had lived here for years." Mitch peeks around the property and admires all the improvements.

Jacob nods. "I said the same thing to myself. It's really crazy. I haven't told this to anyone, but a part of me feels like my uncle knew he was going to pass away. Like he was getting everything ready to leave for me. I get sad thinking about it.

"Mitch makes a lighthearted joke: "I was thinking, you should put some rims and a spoiler on his old Gremlin and drive it around campus."

Shaking his head, Jacob chuckles at that mental image. "Let's go inside. There should be a key in that empty paint bucket on the porch."

As Jacob opens the front door, Mitch shouts, "Whoa! Is this the same house? It looks fuckin' awesome. I can't believe it. Boy did he work hard to get it cleaned up. Incredible. It looks like a different home.

"I know, man. I was blown away when I saw it. He should be here with us doing something inappropriate or disgusting." Jacob suppresses his tears.

Mitch belches. He places his arm around Jacob's shoulder and reassures, "He's here, Jake…he's here."

"Then let's *finally* go check out the basement." Jacob smiles and they high-five.

Jacob tugs the chain hanging from the ceiling at the top of the stairwell. The staircase light turns on but it's dim. A penetrating, musty smell fills the air. The boys are cautious as they walk down each step, gripping the wooden staircase railing. The sun shines through the basement windows and light sparkles on the floor at the bottom of the stairs.

Jacob's mouth falls open. "Wow, it doesn't look like he did any organizing down here. It's literally filled with all the shit that was up-stairs. That son of a gun tricked me."

Mitch finds the bait-and-switch comical. "Well, now we know where he put everything." The boys shuffle through the mountains of furniture and machine fragments. They make their way over to a small, dark workspace area. Dust particles float in the light rays coming through one window, adding to the mystical aura.

The moment overwhelms Jacob. "It feels like a time capsule down here. Everything is *exactly* as he left it. It's a little eerie, to be honest. There's his work bench over there." Jacob points. "I think those boxes stacked along the wall are where his prototypes are stored. He would always box up everything and label it. It was the only thing he was or-ganized with. There should also be a log of some kind here. He would write down his inventions with a short description and the year he cre-ated it."

Mitch is captivated by the workshop. "When it came to his inven-tions, your uncle was like another person." He peers around the room. "This is really amazing to see, Jake. I can't believe how many tools and mechanical parts are here. It almost feels like we stumbled onto the set of a movie production."

Jacob spots several two-inch-thick binders neatly lined up on wooden shelves built above the workbench. Each of them is stuffed with papers. Jacob removes one and begins to flip through the pages.

"Dude, check this out. These look like the binders he would keep all his sketches in. Before he tried to build anything, he would always draw out what the prototype would look like," Jacob explains like a museum tour guide.

Mitch is mesmerized. "You know, it's remarkable to see this. Think about it: you're *literally* holding his hopes and dreams in your hand. Countless hours of commitment and passion. One thing I always loved about your uncle was that he never stopped using his imagination."

"I guess that's what life's about. He used to say to me all the time, "An idea never actioned is an insult to God." Vivid flashbacks rush through Jacob's mind.

"Jeez, that's powerful, man. I need to write that one down." Mitch takes a drafting pencil from the cup. Looking for something to write on, he rummages through the papers scattered on the work bench.

Jacob grabs Mitch's arm. "Hey, be careful. I don't want to mess anything up. He had everything perfectly organized."

Several papers are knocked off the table and land on the floor. Mitch is frantic and scurries to pick them up and organize them into a neat stack.

"Come on, bro. I *just* told you to be careful." Jacob sets the binder back onto the shelf.

Studying the paper on the top of the stack, Mitch is slow to sit down on the stool.

After a minute of silence, Jacob can't contain his curiosity any longer. "What is it? What are you staring at?"

"It looks like your uncle designed some sort of stent—a tiny wire mesh tube. A doctor inserts it into a clogged artery that pumps blood to your heart," Mitch explains.

Jacob scratches his head. "That's crazy. I wonder why he would have been designing something like that. He didn't know anything about those types of things. He was just a goofy gadget inventor."

"Mitch shows Jacob the sketch and corrects him. "You're wrong. Apparently, he knew more than you thought. I mean, he has *everything* meticulously drawn out here. He's got dimensions, weights, material types…It's all listed here."

"Wow. I'm absolutely shocked, man. I never knew my uncle dabbled with medical stuff." Jacob looks at the collection of household contraptions.

Mitch delivers an update. "This doesn't look like any type of stent I've ever seen. He's got some notes written down here. Give me a minute, I want to read through this."

Peering over Mitch's shoulder, Jacob is eager to know more.

"When I went on that campus tour with my father a few weeks ago, I met one of the medical professors. We need to show this to him," Mitch conveys with a sense of urgency. He grabs a drawing storage tube off the shelf, delicately rolls up the sketch, and drops it inside.

"Um, OK. I guess it's good timing since we start school next week." Crossing his arms, Jacob leans back against the work bench.

Mitch's demeanor instantly changes. He grabs Jacob by the arms and looks him in the eyes. "We're doing this tomorrow." Handing the drawing storage tube to Jacob, he wanders away.

Chapter Eleven

Mitch's Dissertation

• The next moning •

With the convertible top down, Mitch and Jacob coast along the highway toward the college campus. The sunrise breaks through the sky as the cool morning wind blows through the boys' hair. Jacob grasps the storage tube with eagerness as they approach their destination.

Arriving at the campus grounds, Mitch turns into the security checkpoint. He hands his license to the officer on duty. After documenting the information, the officer opens the gate and Mitch drives through.

"Another week and we'll have our student IDs…we can just roll right in," Jacob says as they cruise over to the faculty building.

Mitch goes through the game plan as he parks the car. "So, listen, my dad made some calls yesterday. We're meeting with Professor Chu. He's a cardiologist at Saint Christopher Hospital. It's like 15 minutes from here. Anyway, he's a real nice guy. I met him when I did the tour. He's the one I wanna show this sketch to—and all the notes on it."

"What do you think he's going to say?" Jacob questions.

Mitch unbuckles his seat belt. "Let's go find out."

At the front desk, Mitch greets a young, attractive receptionist with a smile. "Good morning. My name is Mitch Glantz. I have an appointment with Professor Chu at 9 o'clock."

"Good morning. Yes, Professor Chu called earlier and said you would be arriving. Just walk up the stairs to your left and his office is on the second floor. It's room 204," the receptionist directs with a smile.

Mitch turns on his charm. "Thanks so much."

The boys begin to banter as they get some distance from the desk. "Bro, she was *totally* checking me out," Mitch whispers.

"She smiles at everyone, Dude. It's her job. Stay focused," Jacob asserts, as he flicks Mitch's earlobe.

Upstairs, Mitch and Jacob are brimming with anticipation as they approach room 204. Jacob takes a deep breath and puts his hand on Mitch's shoulder. "I just want to thank you for this. I'm not exactly sure what you saw in that sketch, but I know my uncle would appreciate you driving all the way down here."

"Let's see what happens. The world might appreciate this." Mitch is confident as he knocks on the door while Jacob paces.

From behind the boys, a man's voice interjects, "I was just getting my coffee. Come on in." The man opens the door.

Mitch extends his hand. "Thank you so much for meeting with us, Professor Chu. We really appreciate you taking the time out of your day."

Professor Chu reciprocates with a firm handshake. "It's my pleasure, Mitch. When your father called me, he said you guys found something you wanted me to take a look at. I'm happy to do so."

"Jake, can you take the drawing out of the tube, please," Mitch requests. Jacob pulls the sketch out and hands it over to Mitch.

"We found this in Jacob's uncle's basement. He was an inventor," Mitch informs. "He passed away recently."

Professor Chu is sympathetic. "I'm sorry to hear that. My condolences to you and your family, Jacob."

"Thank you, Professor. It was a tough loss. My uncle and I were very close. He loved to use his imagination and invent things. He would be blown away that we are even here showing you something he created."

"Well, now you have piqued my interest. Let's have a look at what you brought." Professor Chu puts on his reading glasses. Mitch hands the rolled-up sketch to the professor and then steps back.

Professor Chu sits down at his desk and unrolls the sketch. He places paper weights at the top and bottom of the paper. There is silence as the professor examines the diagram then turns around in his swivel chair. He slides his reading glasses up to his forehead.

"Mitch, when we met a few weeks ago you mentioned that you plan to be a doctor one day. When I spoke to your father, he also mentioned that you have quite a robust portfolio of medical knowledge. So…you tell me…why did you want me to look at this document?" Professor Chu asks as he crosses his arms.

Surprised, Mitch clears his throat. "Well, when I first saw the sketch, I knew it was a stent that would be used to treat coronary artery blockage. I also know that today when a patient has plaque buildup in an artery and blood flow to the heart is compromised, a stent is used to open up that passage." The professor nods. "From what I have read, even though a stent can be a very effective treatment, there are still serious risks associated with having one put in." Mitch pauses and looks at Professor Chu for a sign of approval.

With another nod, the professor instructs, "Keep going."

"Well, a stent can stop working over time due to natural wear of the device itself. The doctor wouldn't know this occurred without a nuclear scan of the arteries. There can also be severe allergic reactions to the stainless steel or cobalt alloy metal. That's a known risk that patients consent to. In addition, there are some cases in which the stent can even cause blood clots. When these types of reactions occur, the stent must be immediately removed. This is a much more invasive procedure than the initial insertion. Unfortunately, once the stent is taken out, the patient is at risk again of coronary blockage."

Professor Chu smiles. "If this were a test, so far you would have passed with flying colors. So, tell me, what was *different* about the stent on that piece of paper you brought me?"

Walking back and forth, Mitch explains, "What if there was a method in which the stent is only in the patient's body for an extremely short amount of time...minutes. It would be inserted through the catheter in the same direction as the patient's natural blood stream." Mitch walks over to the white board, picks up a marker, and begins to illustrate as he speaks. "Doing this would essentially cause the stent to self-propel. Similar to a leaf riding the current of a stream. Then, what if instead of stainless steel or cobalt, the stent is created from an encased gel substance. This would allow the stent to have fluid mobility through the artery, minimizing any strain or trauma to the blood vessel. The stent would have polycarbonate nubs covering the entire circumference. As the stent travels through the artery it begins to break up the plaque lining, eliminating the blockage. Not only does this "plaque destruction" happen upon insertion, but also again when the stent is retrieved back out of the artery. It's a two-for-one treatment for the patient." Mitch grins as he drops the marker back into the tray under the board.

In complete awe, Jacob mumbles, "Holy cow," as he takes a deep breath.

"Mitch, I have been teaching for over 20 years. I am not sure what is more fascinating, the document you brought in today or your interpretation of it. You nailed it. Jacob's uncle would be proud of you. Listen, I would like to make a photocopy of this and show it to one of my colleagues, Dr. Nowak. He is the head of cardiology at Saint Christopher Hospital. He also has done extensive coronary treatment research with some of the most well-known heart surgeons in the world. I want him to validate what you so perfectly articulated today. This could be a game changer, guys," Professor Chu states with a glance to each of his visitors.

Mitch offers his appreciation. "Professor Chu, thank you so much for your time. We are both grateful that you agreed to meet with us. I know how busy you are."

"I thank both of you for uncovering this. As I said, this could be a needle in a haystack, but it's worth investigating further." The Professor escorts the boys to the copy machine.

After making a copy of the document, Professor Chu hands Jacob the tube containing the sketch and states, "I'll be in touch."

The boys each shake the professor's hand and then head back toward the staircase. They high five each other in celebration of Mitch's brilliant dissertation. On the way out of the building, Mitch walks over to the receptionist. Overflowing with confidence, he requests, "Hello. Me again. Do you happen to have a pen and a piece of paper?"

The polite receptionist obliges and hands over both items with a smile. Writing down several words, Mitch then folds the piece of paper in half and slides it over to her. "Have a great day," Mitch announces as he struts away and winks.

Outside, Jacob asks, "What the hell did you write on that piece of paper?"

"I'll tell you if she calls me." Mitch grins.

The boys put their arms around each other's shoulders as they walk to the car.

I always knew in my heart that Mitch was a genius, but that day it was confirmed. It felt like a religious experience listening to him eloquently dissect my uncle's idea the way he did. Not only was it effortless, but he did it with passion. If there was ever a question whether Mitch should pursue his dream of becoming a doctor, it was put to bed that day. I could see the amazement on Professor Chu's face. I'm sure he could also see the admiration in mine. I had no idea that my uncle had such a comprehensive knowledge about medicine.

Apparently, all the books in his basement weren't just for show. You know…if it had all ended when we walked out of the faculty building, I would have been happy. Just hearing someone of significant stature validate one of my uncle's ideas was all I ever wanted.

Chapter Twelve
The "L" Word

• One day later •

Cuddled together on the couch, Christine rests her head on Jacob's chest. She jokes, "I probably could have bought this movie by now with the amount of late fees I'm going to have. My mom is going to kill me. Oh well. Anyway, I can't believe next week our lives change forever."

Jacob runs his fingers through Christine's hair. "I know. It's so hard to comprehend that this time next week we'll both be in different colleges. When I look at that photo album my uncle made me, it doesn't seem that long ago I was that kid sitting on top of his shoulders. I guess we have to just be grateful for each day and not take the people we love for granted." He kisses her forehead. "Like how I feel about you."

"Whoa, hold on! Did you just casually attempt to slide in the 'L word' on me?" Christine jokes as she looks up at Jacob.

Jacob stares back at Christine and utters a confessional, "Oops."

Inching toward Jacob's ear, she whispers, "Well, in that case, I'll make sure I never take *you* for granted. Oops."

The telephone in Jacob's bedroom begins to ring. "Well, that couldn't have been worse timing. I'm so sorry. Do you mind if I go get that real fast? It could be Mitch. He said he would call me if he heard back from Professor Chu." Jacob sits up.

Christine wraps herself inside the fleece blanket draped over the couch. "Of course. Hurry up. Go grab it. That's a call you don't want to miss."

Kissing Christine on the cheek, Jacob gets up and dashes into his bedroom. Grabbing the phone, he answers out of breath, "Hello?"

"Hey, it's me. Listen, did you update your dad on everything that's going on?" Mitch attempts to contain his excitement.

Jacob confirms, "Yeah, Dude. Last night I told him everything. He thinks I was exaggerating when I explained what Professor Chu said."

"Well, your dad is in for a surprise. I spoke to Professor Chu about 30 minutes ago. He's asking if you, your father, and I can all be at his office tomorrow morning at 10 o'clock." Mitch emphasizes the time.

The unexpected news shocks Jacob. "Wow. Yeah, I think so."

"Listen, we *need* to be there. Trust me on this one. I also need you to do me a favor. Remember when I dropped that stack of papers in your uncle's basement?"

Jacob responds, "Yeah, I remember. Why?"

"When I picked them up, I saw at least five or six more sketches that he had done. I told Professor Chu, and he wants you to bring them. Can you get them today?" Mitch is eager for an answer.

"I'm with Christine right now. We're getting ready to watch *My Cousin Vinny*. I can't just leave her here." Jacob bites his nails.

Frustrated, Mitch insists, "Dude, then take her with you. Get those other sketches *today* and bring them tomorrow. Please! Listen, I gotta roll. The Nets are retiring Petrovic's jersey tonight. Pick me up on the way to campus tomorrow. I'll be waiting outside of my house at 9 a.m."

Jacob hangs up the phone and walks back to the couch. He asks Christine, "So, are you up to taking a trip over to my uncle's house?"

"Um, yeah, sure. What's going on?" Christine puts on her flip-flops and stands up.

After a deep breath, Jacob extends his arm. "Pinch me, *please*. I have to be dreaming." He smiles. "Professor Chu wants to see the other sketches we found. I need to go get them. Mitch, my father, and I are going to meet Professor Chu and one of his colleagues tomorrow morning."

"Um…does your father know this?" Christine inquires.

Jacob grabs his car keys. "There's a lot my father doesn't know. But he's going to find out."

Chapter Thirteen

Inventing Belief

• The next morning•

Howard squirms and declares, "I don't know what I'm more shocked about, the fact that I let you drive or that I agreed to go with you two yo-yos."

Looking over at his father, Jacob announces, "Just sit back and relax, big guy. We're here."

Jacob makes eye contact with the officer manning the security booth. The guard recognizes Mitch, smiles and gives him a thumbs up. The gate opens and the car drives through. Jacob zips into a parking space in front of the faculty building. He grabs the drawing tube containing the additional sketches. Everyone bolts out of the car and shuffles toward the entrance.

"Before we go in…. Dad, a few rules so you don't embarrass me. Here they are: number 1. Listen; number 2. Let other people talk; and number 3. *Do not* say anything bad about Uncle O. *Please*," Jacob begs.

"Calm down, pal and stop stressing out. I'm not going to embarrass you." Howard unbuttons his pants and re-tucks his shirt into his underwear.

Mitch holds the entrance door open and everyone funnels inside.

"I got this," Mitch informs as he grins at Jacob and Howard while walking backwards. Spinning around, he sashays toward the receptionist's desk.

Howard can't help but notice, and remarks, "What's with your boy, Casanova?"

"He hasn't told me details yet, but he has a crush on the reception-ist. God only knows what he's saying to her." Jacob finds the soap opera scene humorous.

Gesturing in the air, Mitch waves Howard and Jacob over to the reception desk.

As they approach, Jacob reminds Howard, "Remember, Dad, please *do not* embarrass me."

"Professor Chu is ready to meet with us. Give me the tube with the sketches. He's going to want to see those before we go in and talk to him and Dr. Nowak," Mitch instructs.

Skeptical, Howard shakes his head. "Come on fellas. Are you seri-ous? My brother invented useless things. Nothing worth anything."

Mitch replies, "If that was the case, we wouldn't be here. The peo-ple we're meeting with don't waste their time with amateurs. Let's go, guys."

Rushing up the stairs, Howard is several feet in front of the boys. Mitch whispers to Jacob, "Please make sure your dad behaves himself."

"I've told him *three times* already, man. I know him very well. He is *not* happy that we have even gotten this far." Jacob's stress lev-el is rising like the mercury inside of a thermometer.

As they enter the hallway, Mitch alerts Howard, "It's room 204."

Professor Chu exits his office to greet everyone, "I thought I heard you. Good morning. Thank you all for meeting me on such short notice...Jacob, Mitch, long time no see."

Nudging his way in front of the boys with his hand extended, Jacob's father responds, "Our pleasure, Professor Chu. Happy to be here. The name is Howard...Howard Roth."

With a firm handshake, Professor Chu says, "Mr. Roth. A plea-sure to meet you. My condolences go out to you and your entire fam-ily on the loss of your brother. I am *very* sorry."

Howard's nonchalant response is typical. "Oh, thanks."

"Professor Chu, I brought the other drawings that we had spoken about. Here you go." Mitch hands over the tube.

Professor Chu is excited to learn about the contents. "Thank you, Mitch. If you don't mind, I'm going to pass these over to my colleague, Dr. Nowak, to take a look. Please, have a seat in my office and I will be back in shortly. I have coffee and donuts on my desk for everyone. Please, help yourself."

"Donuts! Sounds great!" Howard broadcasts as he races into the professor's office.

Red-faced, Jacob murmurs, "Thank you," to the professor and then rolls his eyes when he casts his gaze at his father.

"Thanks, Professor Chu. I really appreciate you having Dr. Nowak take a look at them," Mitch shares with genuine gratitude.

The boys walk over to room 204 and open the door. Waving a donut in the air, Howard hollers, "Guys, you gotta try the jelly-filled ones. They're unbelievable!"

"Jesus, Dad, you have jelly all over your face. They are going to be in here soon." Jacob is mortified as he tosses a napkin to his father.

Howard speaks while still chewing, "Calm down, relax, pal. I can't imagine these drawings will end up amounting to anything. Don't get your hopes up."

"Dad, *please* stop! We told you, Professor Chu wouldn't have had us come back if he didn't think this was something important. Try being happy, for Christ's sake. You know Uncle O's dream was to just have *someone* say what he was doing meant something. Since you never did it, I'm just happy someone else finally has!" Jacob snaps back with resentment.

Howard becomes aggressive and points his finger at Jacob. "You don't know what the hell you're talking about, Jacob! You never have! That guy caused me nothing but grief and aggravation, my entire life… so…"

Mitch cuts them off, holding up his hands like a crossing guard stopping traffic. "Guys, please. Talk about this after we leave. We are here for a good reason." He looks at Jacob: "Your uncle…" then he looks at Howard: "your brother…created something that could be *really* important. Let's just agree on that for now and acknowledge how incredible that is. We'll know soon if there's any more to this story or if it ends here."

There's a tap on the door before it creaks open. "I'm sorry, I hope I'm not interrupting." Professor Chu is careful not to startle the three men as he pokes his head into the room.

Mitch is quick to respond. "Not at all. We were just talking about how excited we all are that we're here."

"Perfect. Well, let's discuss a few things. First off this is my colleague, Dr. Nowak." Professor Chu makes the introductions as they both enter.

With a warm smile, Dr. Nowak shakes everyone's hand. "It's a pleasure to meet you all. Thank you so much for coming in to talk with us. We thought it would be more appropriate to discuss everything in person instead of over the phone.

Dr. Nowak walks over and grabs the rolling chair. He slides it in front of the group. He sits down and leans forward. "So, I think at this point everyone is aware of why we are all here. Is that fair to say?" Jacob, Mitch, and Howard all acknowledge with nods. "This is a unique situation. To be entirely transparent, I have never seen anything like this before. We have someone deceased who seems to have created something *very* special—something that has the potential to save lives. Lots of lives." Silence pierces the room as everyone is captivated by each word Dr. Nowak speaks.

"I want to be clear…we are not only talking about the unique design…but also about the medical theory behind it. Let me explain. Today we are able to save a significant number of lives using stent technology. The ability to open up a compromised artery can mean the matter of life and death for millions of patients around the world. What we have *not* been able to solve, is an option for the other millions of people whose body has an acute allergic reaction to the stainless steel or cobalt material. If you are not already aware, this is the material that the stent is created from. When an allergic reaction occurs, the stent has to be removed immediately. The patient relies solely on oral medication to break up the plaque particles. This treatment typically has very minimal success rates. There is roughly an 80 percent chance that the artery will remain blocked and coronary blood supply will be restricted. Clearly you can see there is a gap in treatment at this time. Do you have any questions thus far or shall I continue?"

Mesmerized, Jacob, Mitch, and Howard all say in unison, "No, no questions."

Dr. Nowak nods. "Ok then. I will continue. The question becomes, what is so innovative about what is on that piece of paper that was found in your uncle's basement, Jacob? Why are we all taking time out of our busy schedules to be here today? There are two parts I want to outline for everyone. The first is the composition of the stent. A gel encasement. This would allow the device complete fluid mobility inside the shell of the artery. The best way to explain this would be trying to pull a miniature steel net through a straw versus gliding one made of gel. Which one is going to maneuver through easier, causing less damage to the inside of the straw?"

"The one made with gel," Jacob replies as he takes a deep breath.

Dr. Nowak stands up and walks over to the coffee pot. He fills his cup, walks back and sits down. He confirms, "Precisely. Now imagine that straw is actually an artery, lined inside with a very smooth, delicate tissue. We call that the…"

"Endothelium!" Mitch interjects.

Impressed, Dr. Nowak beams. "Well, I know who to call for my next intern opening. That's exactly right, Mitch. Now, the second part of this has to do with how the stent makes its way through the artery. Because of the lightweight gel composition, your uncle's theory is that it will essentially self-propel as the natural blood flow within the artery moves it. Just like a leaf moving in a downstream current. Right, Mitch?"

Mitch grins, "Yes, exactly."

"The dense gel nubs would delicately brush the inner wall of the endothelium, breaking up the plaque buildup as it travels down the artery." Dr. Nowak sips from his mug. "We believe that using this gel technology could eventually lead to encapsulating medication where the entire stent dissolves within the artery, basically coating the full surface of the endothelium with medication. Like greasing a pan before you cook," Dr. Nowak chuckles and stands up.

Howard crosses his arms and rolls his eyes. "This is *really* hard to digest, Dr. I mean my brother was a quack…a fake…a fraud."

Professor Chu steps forward and clasps his arms behind his back. He locks eyes with Howard and corrects him with conviction, "Mr. Roth, I don't know how to tell you this. To be honest, it's not something I ever envisioned saying in my lifetime." The Professor exhales. "Your brother was a genius."

Howard's jaw drops as he steps backward and sits down. His demeanor softens. He struggles to compose himself and wipes the sweat off of his face with a napkin.

"We looked at the other sketches you brought today, as well. I concur with that statement," Dr. Nowak validates.

Howard's voice shudders. "So, what's next? I mean where do we go from here with this?"

"Well, that's up to Jacob. I was informed that your brother left him his estate and all of the possessions stored inside. I'm certainly not an attorney, but if that is the case, we would need Jacob to direct us. We would be willing to help guide you both on how to bring this to market. Without question, the first thing I recommend is to quickly patent the technology. You *definitely* do not want an idea of this magnitude floating around unprotected. I would even suggest that everyone in this room sign a non-disclosure agreement as soon as possible. From there, a prototype would need to be constructed," Dr. Nowak advises.

Howard's insecurities surface. "I recently developed and launched my own retail product. I went through the process and was able to go from conception to market in just a few months. I'm a wiz at this."

"Mr. Roth, with all due respect, we are talking about something *completely* different here. Something like this could take years until it is on the market as a viable option for patients. The clinical trials alone we have seen take up to several years. We are in for a *long* journey, but we both believe it will be worth it," Professor Chu assures.

Imagine...you're 18 years old and you just found out that you basically inherited a medical invention that could potentially save a lot of people's lives. You would think it would be one of the happiest days of my life. It was actually one of the most uncomfortable. Even after my uncle had passed away, my father *still* couldn't bring himself to give Ostaf any accolades. I'm sure everyone in that room could sense his animosity and jealousy. It was still lingering and something that was secretly tearing my father apart. I was getting ready to leave for college in less than a week and knew I needed his help to bring my uncle's dream to fruition. But before I could even think about having that emotional conversation with my dad, I had to prepare myself to say goodbye to Christine. It wasn't going to be easy.

• One week later •

Jacob parks his car in front of Bagel Land and jokes with Christine, "So, since this will be our last breakfast together for a while, I say we get like *ten* orders of mini muffins."

"Jeez, you make it sound so final." Christine suppresses her tears.

Jacob tries to inject some humor. "Well, just make sure you're not meeting some douchey frat guy for breakfast, OK?"

"*Excuse me*, Mr. Roth? Here's the deal: I promise no frat guys, as long as *you* promise that you won't be going to breakfast with some skanky sorority chick. Got it?" Christine scowls and holds up a playful fist.

Jacob grins. "You know what? That has to be the easiest promise I ever had to make."

Christine caresses Jacob's hand. "I'm really sorry the last few weeks have been so crazy for you. My father always says that life is like a roller coaster: One minute you're looking down at the world and the next you're barreling through it. I'm glad I've been on this ride with you."

Jacob stares at Christine in awe. The sun's golden rays pierce through the car window, reflecting onto her face. Jacob looks into her crystal-blue eyes.

Christine asks, "What are you looking at?" There's silence.

"I'm not religious. But I do believe God puts the perfect person in your life at the *exact* time you need them. I'm not sure I would have been able to get through the last few weeks without you. And what sucks now is that we have to say goodbye." Tears fill Jacob's eyes.

She places her palms onto Jacob's face. "Listen, we may meet new friends and go on some new adventures, but you have my heart. That's all you need to know. Just don't screw it up and I'm yours forever." They both laugh in unison as tears trickle down their faces.

Jacob wipes his eyes. "Do you really believe that?"

Christine runs her nails along Jacob's arm. She clarifies, "Which part? That I'm yours forever or that I think you will screw it up?"

Jacob answers, "That you will be with me forever? I mean, *forever* is a long time."

"Mr. Roth. Look at me. One thing you will learn is that I don't say things I don't mean. Got it?" Christine squeezes Jacob's hand.

Whether it's the joy of a Friday night movie, belly laughing with a best friend, or holding someone's hand for the first time, it's those moments we live for. In those few weeks, I had experienced just about every feeling one could imagine. Even though I was only 18, I knew when a blessing had come into my life. My feelings would always guide me. That was my radar to tell me if I was where I needed to be. I knew Christine was someone who made me a better person.

When my uncle died, it was the first time I had experienced the pain of having to say goodbye to someone I never wanted to leave. The finality was what hurt the most. At the same time, it helped me to understand the blessings that were right in front of me. I saw them, embraced them, and appreciated them. Knowing where I stood with Christine was a huge relief. It was then time to find out exactly where I stood with my father. It wasn't going to be easy; he was stubborn, a know-it-all, and someone who would never admit when he made a mistake. But I was ready to confront him.

Chapter Fourteen

Onboard with Fate

• Later that night •

Like a police raid, Howard bangs on Jacob's bedroom door and then bolts into the room. "What's going on, Jake?"

"Jeez, Dad, you scared the crap out of me. I'm just packing the last couple of duffel bags."

Howard can't contain his excitement. "I have got some really sensational news, pal. I just found out that Joe Namath is going to be endorsing the Cool-It Sports Drink Bottle. This is huge! Are you kidding me? The guy is an icon. Want to know the best part?"

Jacob plays along: "Sure, Dad. Tell me, what's the best part?" His sarcasm goes unnoticed.

Bubbling, Howard shares, "We are going to be shooting a commercial at his house in Tequesta, Florida. You get to be in it! Not only that—it gets better. You get to pick a friend to be in it with you. We could fly down on a weekend to film it."

"That's really cool, Dad. It's too bad that Uncle O isn't around to hear that news. Man, he *loved* Broadway Joe. He would have been excited to know that." Memories of watching New York Jets games with Ostaf flash through Jacob's mind.

Howard scoffs and corrects his son. "I doubt that, Jacob. Maybe angry...jealous...irritated...but definitely not excited. He was never happy to hear that something good happened in my life. He could never just say, 'Nice job.' My brother always wanted something, even if he had absolutely nothing to do with working hard to create it."

Jacob steps forward. "I understand, Dad, but the past has already been written. Last I checked you can't change it. He was who he was, like you always tell me. Uncle O wasn't perfect by any means. I know that. He would drive me crazy, too, but he did the best he could. In the end, that's really all you can expect from someone. Everyone has their own struggles and challenges. I have mine, you have yours, mom has hers, we all do. It's time to let the frustration and anger go, Dad... please."

"You're wise beyond your years, pal. There's a small part of me that agrees with you," Howard admits as he takes a deep breath.

Jacob is dumbfounded. "Holy shit! Did you just say that you agree with me?"

Howard can't hide his smirk. "Please don't tell anyone. I have to protect my reputation, you know. Listen, Jakester, I have been thinking a lot about everything that is going on. My business, you leaving for school, and Ostaf's invention..."

Jacob interrupts: "I really want to talk to you about that last one."

"Relax and hear me out. I know you're leaving and you will be focused on school and starting a new life on campus. That's exactly what I want you to do...and that's what your uncle would want you to do." Howard sits down on the edge of the bed.

Jacob calms down. "Thanks, Dad. I appreciate that."

"Listen, you better not be recording me, because I am going to admit that I agree with you again." Howard grins. "Life challenges affect everyone differently. When my father died, it broke my spirit— there is no other way to say it. I had my own struggles getting over the shock of losing him at such a young age. As much as it crushed me, it absolutely devastated my brother. He was never able to recover. It's easy to judge other people, Jacob."

Jacob sits next to his father and puts his arm around his shoulder.

Howard delivers the unexpected news. "I'm going to help do what I can to bring my brother's dream to life. I'm not sure what will come of it, but I'll do everything I can to support Dr. Nowak and Professor Chu."

Jacob's jaw drops open and he places his hand on his forehead. "Are you serious, Dad? That's amazing. I don't even know what to say."

Howard's face is solemn as he embraces his son. "There's nothing you have to say." At peace, Jacob leans his head on his father and utters, "Thank you."

I never imagined that conversation would go the way it did. My father's vulnerability blew me away. That night was the only time I ever remember him admitting he was wrong. But in the same breath, he was also right. It's so easy to judge others. It's our natural reaction to deal with our own insecurities, failures, and regrets. So much of our lives are spent wasting our valuable energy dissecting the actions of other people. Imagine if we invested that time building our own legacy. We are all born into circumstances we can't control. When we understand that, we can start to build each other up instead of tear each other down. It's unfortunate that my father came to that realization after my uncle died, but I was grateful that he finally did.

I was leaving for college with a full heart, knowing I could hand off my uncle's dream to someone who cared about it. It was time to close the book on the summer of 1993. It was one I will never forget—one that changed my life forever, but there was one more thing I had to do.

Chapter Fifteen
Imagination Validation

• Star of David Cemetary •

A re you sure you don't want me to come with you?" Christine caresses Jacob's back.

Swallowing hard, Jacob wipes his clammy palms on his pants. "Thank you, but I need to do this by myself." He unbuckles his seat belt and exits the car.

In the distance he sees clusters of headstones lining the manicured grass. The sky is overcast and gray. The smell of the approaching rainstorm drifts through the air as Jacob trudges toward the gravesite. Memories race through his mind. Like a movie projector, Jacob vividly recalls the recent summer visits he had with his uncle. He scans the markers looking for Ostaf's name.

"Where are you hiding, Uncle O?" Jacob whispers. He tiptoes in between the plots trying to be respectful of where he steps. When he sees his uncle's headstone, he kneels down, grabs a rock and speaks aloud: "I thought I would never find you. The last time I stood here was a blur to me. I'm surprised I was even in the right part of this cemetery. They sure do keep this place looking nice. Before I leave, I'm going to stop by and say hi to Grandpa. He would be so proud of you."

Jacob places the rock atop the headstone, as a sign he'd been there. "So, I just wanted to give you an update on everything that has happened." Jacob exhales. "I leave for school this afternoon. It's hard to believe how fast this summer blew by. Things are going good with Christine. Luckily, I haven't screwed it up yet." Jacob chuckles. "It's going to suck that I won't be seeing her every day. I just pray that things between us don't change, but you never know." Subtle sounds of thunder rumble in the distance.

Jacob's voice begins to flutter as emotions overtake him. "The last 2 weeks I've done a lot of thinking about life and the purpose of why we're here. I know that's probably a little odd being that I'm so young. But losing you changed my perspective on a lot of things. You taught me so much. One lesson that I'll always remember is the power of believing. You always believed. It didn't matter what anyone else said. You kept creating and imagining and never quit. You actually had the nerve to dream that a high school dropout with a learning disability could change the world. It's going to happen, Uncle O. I know it... I believe it. Rest easy, big guy. I love you, forever."

After that day, I would visit my uncle's gravesite whenever I was home from college. I knew his physical body was there, but his soul followed me wherever I went. It's hard to explain, but I could almost feel someone pick me up and spiritually push me toward the things I was hesitant to do—like I was being guided. I knew he was watching over me and always would be.

Christine and I survived our first two years of college as a couple. Unfortunately, things didn't work out the way we thought they would. The stress of attending different schools eventually took its toll. We stayed friends, but after we graduated, we went our separate ways. I'll always be grateful for the wonderful times we shared.

I ended up staying in Northern New Jersey. After six years of being a teacher I was given the opportunity to become an elementary school principal. Early in my career, I was given the chance to work in what some would call "high risk" schools. It was the best decision I ever made. Making an impact on the life of a student who had never been blessed with a positive role model was the ultimate reward. Like Mitch once told me, when you love something, it's never work…and if someone is willing to pay me to do something that I would do for free…then I guess I did end up winning the game of life.

Speaking of Mitch…well, he never got a call from the receptionist in the faculty building. He was the best man at my wedding and ended up marrying one of my wife's bridesmaids. In between renters, we still go back to my uncle's house with our own families for holidays. That is, of course, when he isn't working in the emergency room. Last June, he became the head of cardiology at Saint Christopher Hospital when Dr. Nowak retired.

My father's Cool-It Sports Drink Bottle was a short-lived success. About a year after the product hit the market, three other companies caught onto the technology and created slightly different versions. They had the financial backing and access to supply chains that could scale the product at a much more cost-effective price per unit. Within 16 months there were at least five different variations of the product on the market. There was nothing "special" about my father's invention anymore. We were fortunate that he had made a lot of money off the initial orders. That gave him the time and financial freedom to spend the next year working with the doctors to bring my uncle's creation to life.

Right after the prototype was created, the dissolvable gel-encased stent was patented and rollout began quickly for clinical trials. The technology was proven to be a game-changer in the treatment for coronary blockage. It was purchased by a major pharmaceutical company and soon after, distributed worldwide.

So, I guess you could *technically* say my Uncle O ended up changing the world. One of his wacky, quirky ideas has already saved a few million lives…including mine.

• The End •

Epilogue

Because I wanted this story to be anchored around those who view the world differently than most, I began to recognize how lucky I was growing up with characters like that in my own life. Some of those people worked hard to turn their visions into realities while others just spoke about their never-fulfilled plans.

My father demonstrated that creativity bundled with effort could bring ideas to fruition. He attacked life…seized each day with passion and intensity. He showed me that you can love your traditional day job, be great at it, and then work hard on your passion projects at night. He was polished, focused, and bubbling with energy—a dream chaser. Inspired by my beloved father, Larry Shapiro, the character Howard Roth was created.

Writing a story anchored around the power of believing, I tried to capture that one unusual family member…you know, the quirky one who is never embraced or taken seriously. This person saw everything from an unconventional perspective. He often didn't show up for family gatherings or celebrations, sometimes not even invited. This eccentric, outcast individual was the catalyst for my character Ostaf Roth.

As the story began to come to life, so did Jacob and Ostaf's relationship. It was built upon friendship, trust, and forgiveness. The type of bond that would carry on forever. I began to actually feel the power of their personalities. The love, understanding, and acceptance Jacob had for his uncle was truly remarkable. I was reminded of friendships that I have had in my own life. Before I knew it, this magical relationship had captivated me.

The characters I created actually ended up inspiring *me*. They pushed me to use my imagination and creativity while writing this story. They made me believe my dream of publishing this book could come true. In the end, Jacob, Howard, and Ostaf *showed me* that my imagination could maybe help motivate others to create positive change in the world.

Dedication

This book is dedicated to my father, Lawrence Peter Shapiro.

On March 11, 2013, he unexpectedly passed away, but his electric spirit, tenacious work ethic, and zest for life, will never be forgotten.